A CRYSTAL AGE

William Henry Hudson was born in 1841 near Buenos Aires, Argentina of American parents. Spending his childhood and youth on the pampas studying the flora and fauna, he became an authority on ornithology. He travelled extensively in South America, but after developing a heart condition he emigrated to England around 1869.

Hudson was a keen observer and lover of nature, particularly of birds, and he was one of the founder members of the Royal Society for the Protection of Birds (RSPB) in the UK. His works include a series of books on the natural history of South America and England, although his best known work, *Green Mansions* (1904), is a romance set in the South American jungle.

A Crystal Age, first published in 1887, is Hudson's view of a future where man has returned to a forest state, living in small communities in harmony with nature.

A Crystal Age

W. H. Hudson

FrontList Books

Published by FrontList Books.
An imprint of Soft Editions Ltd,
Gullane, East Lothian, Scotland.

First published 1887.

ISBN 1-84350-080-9

A Crystal Age

Then gin I thinke on that which Nature sayd,
Of that same time when no more change shall be
But stedfast rest of all things firmely stayd
Upon the pillours of Eternity.

PREFACE TO THE SECOND EDITION

ROMANCES of the future, however fantastic they may be, have for most of us a perennial if mild interest, since they are born of a very common feeling—a sense of dissatisfaction with the existing order of things, combined with a vague faith in or hope of a better one to come. The picture put before us is false; we knew it would be false before looking at it, since we cannot imagine what is unknown any more than we can build without materials. Our mental atmosphere surrounds and shuts us in like our own skins; no one can boast that he has broken out of that prison. The vast, unbounded prospect lies before us, but, as the poet mournfully adds, "clouds and darkness rest upon it." Nevertheless we cannot suppress all curiosity, or help asking one another, What is *your* dream—your ideal? What is your News from Nowhere, or, rather, what is the result of the little shake *your* hand has given to the old pasteboard toy with a dozen bits of coloured glass for contents? And, most important of all, can you present it in a narrative or romance which will enable me to pass an idle hour not disagreeably? How, for instance, does it compare in this respect with other prophetic books on the shelf?

I am not referring to living authors; least of all to that flamingo of letters who for the last decade or so has been a wonder to our island birds. For what could I say of him that is not known to every one—that he is the tallest of fowls, land or water, of a most singular shape, and has black-tipped crimson wings folded under his delicate rose-coloured plumage? These other books referred to, written, let us say, from thirty or forty years to a century or two ago, amuse us in a way their poor dead authors never intended. Most amusing are the dead ones who take themselves seriously, whose books are pulpits quaintly carved and decorated with precious stones and silken canopies in which they stand and preach to or at their contemporaries.

In like manner, in going through this book of mine after so many years I am amused at the way it is coloured by the little cults and crazes, and modes of thought of the 'eighties of the last century. They were so important then, and now, if remembered at all, they appear so trivial! It pleases me to be diverted in this way at "A Crystal Age"—to find, in fact, that I have not stood still while the world has been moving.

This criticism refers to the case, the habit, of the book rather than to its spirit, since when we write we do, as the red man thought, impart something of our souls to the paper, and it is probable that if I were to write a new dream of the future it would, though in some respects very different from this, still be a dream and picture of the human race in its forest period.

Alas that in this case the wish cannot induce belief! For now I remember another thing which Nature said—that earthly excellence can come in no way but one, and the ending of passion and strife is the beginning of decay. It is indeed a hard saying, and the hardest lesson we can learn of her without losing love and bidding good-bye for ever to hope.

W. H. H.
September 1906.

I

I DO not quite know how it happened, my recollection of the whole matter being in a somewhat clouded condition. I fancy I had gone somewhere on a botanising expedition, but whether at home or abroad I don't know. At all events, I remember that I had taken up the study of plants with a good deal of enthusiasm, and that while hunting for some variety in the mountains I sat down to rest on the edge of a ravine. Perhaps it was on the ledge of an overhanging rock; anyhow, if I remember rightly, the ground gave way all about me, precipitating me below. The fall was a very considerable one—probably thirty or forty feet, or more, and I was rendered unconscious. How long I lay there under the heap of earth and stones carried down in my fall it is impossible to say: perhaps a long time; but at last I came to myself and struggled up from the *débris*, like a mole coming to the surface of the earth to feel the genial sunshine on his dim eyeballs. I found myself standing (oddly enough, on all fours) in an immense pit created by the overthrow of a gigantic dead tree with a girth of about thirty or forty feet. The tree itself had rolled down to the bottom of the ravine; but the pit in which it had left the huge stumps of severed roots was, I found, situated in a gentle slope at the top of the bank! How, then, I could have fallen seemingly so far from no height at all, puzzled me greatly: it looked as if the solid earth had been indulging in some curious transformation pranks during those moments or minutes of insensibility. Another singular circumstance was that I had a great mass of small fibrous rootlets tightly woven about my whole person, so that I was like a colossal basket-worm in its case, or a big man-shaped bottle covered with wicker-work. It appeared as if the roots had *grown* round me! Luckily they were quite sapless and brittle, and without bothering my brains too much about the matter, I set to work to rid myself of them. After stripping the woody covering off, I found that my tourist suit of rough Scotch homespun had not suffered much harm, although the cloth exuded a damp, mouldy smell; also that my thick-soled climbing boots had assumed a cracked rusty appearance as if I had been engaged in some brick-field operations; while my felt hat was in such a discoloured and battered condition that I felt almost ashamed to put it on my head. My watch was gone; perhaps I had not been wearing it, but my pocket-book in which I had my money was safe in my breast pocket.

Glad and grateful at having escaped with unbroken bones from such a dangerous accident, I set out walking along the edge of the ravine, which soon broadened to a valley running between two steep hills; and then, seeing water at the bottom and feeling very dry, I ran down the slope to get a drink. Lying flat on my chest to slake my thirst animal fashion, I was amazed at the reflection the water gave back of my face: it was, skin and hair, thickly encrusted with clay and rootlets! Having taken a long drink, I threw off my clothes to have a bath; and after splashing about for half an hour managed to rid my skin of its accumulations of dirt. While drying in the wind I shook the loose sand and clay from my garments, then dressed, and, feeling greatly refreshed, proceeded on my walk.

For an hour or so I followed the valley in its many windings, but, failing to see any dwelling-place, I ascended a hill to get a view of the surrounding country. The prospect which disclosed itself when I had got a couple of hundred feet above the surrounding level, appeared unfamiliar. The hills among which I had been wandering were now behind me; before me spread a wide rolling country, beyond which rose a mountain range resembling in the distance blue banked-up clouds with summits and peaks of pearly whiteness. Looking on this scene I could hardly refrain from shouting with joy, so glad did the sunlit expanse of earth, and the pure exhilarating mountain breeze, make me feel. The season was late summer—that was plain to see; the ground was moist, as if from recent showers, and the earth everywhere had that intense living greenness with which it reclothes itself when the greater heats are over; but the foliage of the woods was already beginning to be touched here and there with the yellow and russet hues of decay. A more tranquil and soul-satisfying scene could not be imagined: the dear old mother earth was looking her very best; while the shifting golden sunlight, the mysterious haze in the distance, and the glint of a wide stream not very far off, seemed to spiritualise her "happy autumn fields," and bring them into a closer kinship with the blue over-arching sky. There was one large house or mansion in sight, but no town, nor even a hamlet, and not one solitary spire. In vain I scanned the horizon, waiting impatiently to see the distant puff of white steam from some passing engine. This troubled me not a little, for I had no idea that I had drifted so far from civilisation in my search for specimens, or whatever it was that brought me to this pretty, primitive wilderness. Not quite a wilderness, however, for there, within a short hour's walk of the hill, stood the one great stone mansion, close to the river I have mentioned. There were also horses and cows in sight, and a number of scattered sheep were grazing on the hillside beneath me.

Strange to relate, I met with a little misadventure on account of the sheep—an animal which one is accustomed to regard as of a timid and inoffensive nature. When I set out at a brisk pace to walk to the house I have spoken of, in order to make some enquiries there, a few of the sheep that happened to be near began to bleat loudly, as if alarmed, and by and by they came hurrying after me, apparently in a great state of excitement. I did not mind them much, but presently a pair of horses, attracted by their bleatings, also seemed struck at my appearance, and came at a swift gallop to within twenty yards of me. They were magnificent-looking brutes, evidently a pair of well-groomed carriage horses, for their coats, which were of a fine bronze colour, sparkled wonderfully in the sunshine. In other respects they were very unlike carriage animals, for they had tails reaching to the ground, like funeral horses, and immense black leonine manes, which gave them a strikingly bold and somewhat formidable appearance. For some moments they stood with heads erect, gazing fixedly at me, and then simultaneously delivered a snort of defiance or astonishment, so loud and sudden that it startled me like the report of a gun. This tremendous equine blast brought yet another enemy on the field in the shape of a huge milk-white bull with long horns: a very noble kind of animal, but one which I always prefer to admire from behind a hedge, or at a distance through a field-glass. Fortunately his wrathful mutterings gave me timely notice of his approach, and without waiting to discover his intentions, I incontinently fled down the slope to the refuge of a grove or belt of trees clothing the lower portion of the hillside. Spent and panting from my run, I embraced a big tree, and turning to face the foe, found that I had not been followed: sheep, horses, and bull were all grouped together just where I had left them, apparently holding a consultation, or comparing notes.

The trees where I had sought shelter were old, and grew here and there, singly or in scattered groups: it was a pretty wilderness of mingled tree, shrub and flower. I was surprised to find here some very large and ancient-looking fig-trees, and numbers of wasps and flies were busy feeding on a few over-ripe figs on the higher branches. Honey-bees also roamed about everywhere, extracting sweets from the autumn bloom, and filling the sunny glades with a soft, monotonous murmur of sound. Walking on full of happy thoughts and a keen sense of the sweetness of life pervading me, I presently noticed that a multitude of small birds were gathering about me, flitting through the trees overhead and the bushes on either hand, but always keeping near me, apparently as much excited at my presence as if I had been a gigantic owl, or some such unnatural monster. Their increasing numbers and incessant excited chirping and chattering at first served to amuse, but in the end began to irritate me. I observed, too, that the alarm was spreading, and that larger birds, usually shy of men—pigeons, jays, and magpies, I fancied they were—now began to make their appearance. Could it be, thought I with some concern, that I had wandered into some uninhabited wilderness, to cause so great a commotion among the little feathered people? I very soon dismissed this as an idle thought, for one does not find houses, domestic animals, and fruit-trees in desert places. No, it was simply the inherent cantankerousness of little birds which caused them to annoy me. Looking about on the ground for something to throw at them, I found in the grass a freshly-fallen walnut, and, breaking the shell, I quickly ate the contents. Never had anything tasted so pleasant to me before! But it had a curious effect on me, for, whereas before eating it I had not felt hungry, I now seemed to be famishing, and began excitedly searching about for more nuts. They were lying everywhere in the greatest abundance; for, without knowing it, I had been walking through a grove composed in large part of old walnut-trees. Nut after nut was picked up and eagerly devoured, and I must have eaten four or five dozen before my ravenous appetite was thoroughly appeased. During this feast I had paid no attention to the birds, but when my hunger was over I began again to feel annoyed at their trivial persecutions, and so continued to gather the fallen nuts to throw at them. It amused and piqued me at the same time to see how wide of the mark my missiles went. I could hardly have hit a haystack at a distance of ten yards. After half an hour's vigorous practice my right hand began to recover its lost cunning, and I was at last greatly delighted when one of my nuts went hissing like a bullet through the leaves, not further than a yard from the wren, or whatever the little beggar was, I had aimed at. Their Impertinences did not like this at all; they began to find out that I was a rather dangerous person to meddle with: their ranks were broken, they became demoralised and scattered, in all directions, and I was finally left master of the field.

"Dolt that I am!" I suddenly exclaimed, "to be fooling away my time when the nearest railway station or hotel is perhaps twenty miles away."

I hurried on, but when I got to the end of the grove, on the green sward near some laurel and juniper bushes, I came on an excavation apparently just made, the loose earth which had been dug out looking quite fresh and moist. The hole or foss was narrow, about five feet deep and seven feet long, and looked, I imagined, curiously like a grave. A few yards away was a pile of dry brushwood, and some faggots bound together with ropes of straw, all apparently freshly cut from the neighbouring bushes. As I stood there, wondering what these things meant, I happened to glance away in the direction of the house where I intended to call, which was not now visible owing to an intervening grove of tall trees, and was surprised to discover a troop of about fifteen persons advancing along the valley in my direction. Before them marched a tall white-bearded old man; next came eight men, bearing a platform on their shoulders with some heavy burden resting upon it; and behind these followed the others. I began to think that they were actually carrying a corpse, with the intention of giving it burial in that very pit beside which I was standing; and, although it looked most unlike a funeral, for no person in the procession wore black, the thought strengthened to a conviction when I became able to distinguish a recumbent, human-like form in a shroud-like covering on the platform. It seemed altogether a very unusual proceeding, and made me feel extremely uncomfortable; so much so that I considered it prudent to step back behind the bushes, where I could watch the doings of the processionists without being observed.

Led by the old man—who carried, suspended by thin chains, a large bronze censer, or brazier rather, which sent out a thin continuous wreath of smoke—they came straight on to the pit; and after depositing their burden on the grass, remained standing for some minutes, apparently to rest after their walk, all conversing together, but in subdued tones, so that I could not catch their words, although standing within fifteen yards of the grave. The uncoffined corpse, which seemed that of a full-grown man, was covered with a white cloth, and rested on a thick straw mat, provided with handles along the sides. On these things, however, I bestowed but a hasty glance, so profoundly absorbed had I become in watching the group of living human beings before me; for they were certainly utterly unlike any fellow-creatures I had ever encountered before. The old man was tall and spare, and from his snowy-white majestic beard I took him to be about seventy years old; but he was straight as an arrow, and his free movements and elastic tread were those of a much younger man. His head was adorned with a dark red skull-cap, and he wore a robe covering the whole body and reaching to the ankles, of a deep yellow or rhubarb colour; but his long wide sleeves under his robe were dark red, embroidered with yellow flowers. The other men had no covering on their heads, and their luxuriant hair, worn to the shoulders, was, in most cases, very dark. Their garments were also made in a different fashion, and consisted of a kilt-like dress, which came half-way to the knees, a pale yellow shirt fitting tight to the skin, and over it a loose sleeveless vest. The entire legs were cased in stockings, curious in pattern and colour. The women wore garments resembling those of the men, but the tight-fitting sleeves reached only half-way to the elbow, the rest of the arm being bare; and the outer garment was all in one piece, resembling a long sleeveless jacket, reaching below the hips. The colour of their dresses varied, but in most cases different shades of blue and subdued yellow predominated. In all, the stockings showed deeper and richer shades of colour than the other garments; and in their curiously segmented appearance, and in the harmonious arrangement of the tints, they seemed to represent the skins of pythons and other beautifully variegated serpents. All wore low shoes of an orange-brown colour, fitting closely so as to display the shape of the foot.

From the moment of first seeing them I had had no doubt about the sex of the tall old leader of the procession, his shining white beard being as conspicuous at a distance as a shield or a banner; but looking at the others I was at first puzzled to know whether the party was composed of men or women, or of both, so much did they resemble each other in height, in their smooth faces, and in the length of their hair. On a closer inspection I noticed the difference of dress of the sexes; also that the men, if not sterner, had faces at all events less mild and soft in expression than the women, and also a slight perceptible down on the cheeks and upper lip.

After a first hasty survey of the group in general, I had eyes for only one person in it—a fine graceful girl about fourteen years old, and the youngest by far of the party. A description of this girl will give some idea, albeit a very poor one, of the faces and general appearance of this strange people I had stumbled on. Her dress, if a garment so brief can be called a dress, showed a slaty-blue pattern on a straw-coloured ground, while her stockings were darker shades of the same colours. Her eyes, at the distance I stood from her, appeared black, or nearly black, but when seen closely they proved to be green—a wonderfully pure, tender sea-green; and the others, I found, had eyes of the same hue. Her hair fell to her shoulders; but it was very wavy or curly, and strayed in small tendril-like tresses over her neck, forehead and cheeks; in colour it was golden black—that is, black in shade, but when touched with sunlight every hair became a thread of shining red-gold; and in some lights it looked like raven-black hair powdered with gold-dust. As to her features, the forehead was broader and lower, the nose larger, and the lips more slender, than in our most beautiful female types. The colour was also different, the delicately moulded mouth being purple-red instead of the approved cherry or coral hue; while the complexion was a clear dark, and the colour, which mantled the cheeks in moments of excitement, was a dim or dusky rather than a rosy red.

The exquisite form and face of this young girl, from the first moment of seeing her, produced a very deep impression; and I continued watching her every movement and gesture with an intense, even a passionate interest. She had a quantity of flowers in her hand; but these sweet emblems, I observed, were all gaily coloured, which seemed strange, for in most places white flowers are used in funeral ceremonies. Some of the men who had followed the body carried in their hands broad, three-cornered bronze shovels, with short black handles, and these they had dropped upon the grass on arriving at the grave. Presently the old man stooped and drew the covering back from the dead one's face—a rigid, marble-white face set in a loose mass of black hair. The others gathered round, and some standing, others kneeling, bent on the still countenance before them a long earnest gaze, as if taking an eternal farewell of one they had deeply loved. At this moment the beautiful girl I have described all at once threw herself with a sobbing cry on her knees before the corpse, and, stooping, kissed the face with passionate grief. "Oh, my beloved, must we now leave you alone for ever!" she cried between the sobs that shook her whole frame. "Oh, my love—my love—my love, will you come back to us no more!"

The others all appeared deeply affected at her grief, and presently a young man standing by raised her from the ground and drew her gently against his side, where for some minutes she continued convulsively weeping. Some of the other men now passed ropes through the handles of the straw mat on which the corpse rested, and raising it from the platform lowered it into the foss. Each person in turn then advanced and dropped some flowers into the grave, uttering the one word "Farewell" as they did so; after which the loose earth was shovelled in with the bronze implements. Over the mound the hurdle on which the straw mat had rested was then placed, the dry brushwood and faggots heaped over it and ignited with a coal from the brazier. White smoke and crackling flames issued anon from the pile, and in a few moments the whole was in a fierce blaze.

Standing around they all waited in silence until the fire had burnt itself out; then the old man advancing stretched his arms above the white and still smoking ashes and cried in a loud voice: "Farewell for ever, O well beloved son! With deep sorrow and tears we have given you back to Earth; but not until she has made the sweet grass and flowers grow again on this spot, scorched and made desolate with fire, shall our hearts be healed of their wound and forget their grief."

II

THE thrilling, pathetic tone in which these words were uttered affected me not a little; and when the ceremony was over I continued staring vacantly at the speaker, ignorant of the fact that the beautiful young girl had her wide-open, startled eyes fixed on the bush which, I vainly imagined, concealed me from view.

All at once she cried out: "Oh, father, look there! Who is that strange-looking man watching us from behind the bushes?"

They all turned, and then I felt that fourteen or fifteen pairs of very keen eyes were on me, seeing me very plainly indeed, for in my curiosity and excitement I had come out from the thicker bushes to place myself behind a ragged, almost leafless shrub, which afforded the merest apology for a shelter. Putting a bold face on the matter, although I did not feel very easy, I came out and advanced to them, removing my battered old hat on the way, and bowing repeatedly to the assembled company. My courteous salutation was not returned; but all, with increasing astonishment pictured on their faces, continued staring at me as if they were looking on some grotesque apparition. Thinking it best to give an account of myself at once, and to apologise for intruding on their mysteries, I addressed myself to the old man:

"I really beg your pardon," I said, "for having disturbed you at such an inconvenient time, and while you are engaged in these—these solemn rites; but I assure you, sir, it has been quite accidental. I happened to be walking here when I saw you coming, and thought it best to step out of the way until—well, until the funeral was over. The fact is, I met with a serious accident in the mountains over there. I fell down into a ravine, and a great heap of earth and stones fell on and stunned me, and I do not know how long I lay there before I recovered my senses. I daresay I am trespassing, but I am a perfect stranger here, and quite lost, and—and perhaps a little confused after my fall, and perhaps you will kindly tell me where to go to get some refreshment, and find out where I am."

"Your story is a very strange one," said the old man in reply, after a pause of considerable duration. "That you are a perfect stranger in this place is evident from your appearance, your uncouth dress, and your thick speech."

His words made me blush hotly, although I should not have minded his very personal remarks much if that beautiful girl had not been standing there listening to everything. My *uncouth* garments, by the way, were made by a fashionable West End tailor, and fitted me perfectly, although just now they were, of course, very dirty. It was also a surprise to hear that I had a *thick speech*, since I had always been considered a remarkably clear speaker and good singer, and had frequently both sung and recited in public, at amateur entertainments.

After a distressing interval of silence, during which they all continued regarding me with unabated curiosity, the old gentleman condescended to address me again and asked me my name and country.

"My country," said I, with the natural pride of a Briton, "is England, and my name is Smith."

"No such country is known to me," he returned; "nor have I ever heard such a name as yours."

I was rather taken aback at his words, and yet did not just then by any means realise their full import. I was thinking only about my name; for without having penetrated into any perfectly savage country, I had been about the world a great deal for a young man, visiting the Colonies, India, Yokohama, and other distant places, and I had never yet been told that the name of Smith was an unfamiliar one.

"I hardly know what to say," I returned, for he was evidently waiting for me to add something more to what I had stated. "It rather staggers me to hear that my name—well, you have not heard of *me*, of course, but there have been a great many distinguished men of the same name: Sydney Smith, for instance, and—and several others." It mortified me just then to find that I had forgotten all the other distinguished Smiths.

He shook his head, and continued watching my face.

"Not heard of them!" I exclaimed. "Well, I suppose you have

heard of some of my great countrymen: Beaconsfield, Gladstone, Darwin, Burne-Jones, Ruskin, Queen Victoria, Tennyson, George Eliot, Herbert Spencer, General Gordon, Lord Randolph Churchill——"

As he continued to shake his head after each name I at length paused.

"Who are all these people you have named?" he asked.

"They are all great and illustrious men and women who have a world-wide reputation," I answered.

"And are there no more of them—have you told me the names of *all* the great people you have ever known or heard of?" he said, with a curious smile.

"No, indeed," I answered, nettled at his words and manner. "It would take me until to-morrow to name *all* the great men I have ever heard of. I suppose you have heard the names of Napoleon, Wellington, Nelson, Dante, Luther, Calvin, Bismarck, Voltaire?"

He still shook his head.

"Well, then," I continued, "Homer, Socrates, Alexander the Great, Confucius, Zoroaster, Plato, Shakespeare." Then, growing thoroughly desperate, I added in a burst: "Noah, Moses, Columbus, Hannibal, Adam and Eve!"

"I am quite sure that I have never heard of any of these names," he answered, still with that curious smile. "Nevertheless I can understand your surprise. It sometimes happens that the mind, owing to an imperfect adjustment of its faculties, resembles the uneducated vision in its method of judgment, regarding the things which are near as great and important, and those further away as less important, according to their distance. In such a case the individuals one hears about or associates with, come to be looked upon as the great and illustrious beings of the world, and all men in all places are expected to be familiar with their names. But come, my children, our sorrowful task is over, let us now return to the house. Come with us, Smith, and you shall have the refreshment you require."

I was, of course, pleased with the invitation, but did not relish being addressed as "Smith," like some mere labourer or other common person tramping about the country.

The long disconcerting scrutiny I had been subjected to had

naturally made me very uncomfortable, and caused me to drop a little behind the others as we walked towards the house. The old man, however, still kept at my side; but whether from motives of courtesy, or because he wished to badger me a little more about my uncouth appearance and defective intellect, I was not sure. I was not anxious to continue the conversation, which had not proved very satisfactory; moreover, the beautiful girl I have already mentioned so frequently, was now walking just before me, hand in hand with the young man who had raised her from the ground. I was absorbed in admiration of her graceful figure, and—shall I be forgiven for mentioning such a detail?—her exquisitely rounded legs under her brief and beautiful garments. To my mind the garment was quite long enough. Every time I spoke, for my companion still maintained the conversation and I was obliged to reply, she hung back a little to catch my words. At such times she would also turn her pretty head partially round so as to see me: then her glances, beginning at my face, would wander down to my legs, and her lips would twitch and curl a little, seeming to express disgust and amusement at the same time. I was beginning to hate my legs, or rather my trousers, for I considered that under them I had as good a pair of calves as any man in the company.

Presently I thought of something to say, something very simple, which my dignified old friend would be able to answer without intimating that he considered me a wild man of the woods or an escaped lunatic.

"Can you tell me," I said pleasantly, "what is the name of your nearest town or city? how far it is from this place, and how I can get there?"

At this question, or series of questions, the young girl turned quite round, and, waiting until I was even with her, she continued her walk at my side, although still holding her companion's hand.

The old man looked at me with a grave smile—that smile was fast becoming intolerable—and said: "Are you so fond of honey, Smith? You shall have as much as you require without disturbing the bees. They are now taking advantage of this second spring to lay by a sufficient provision before winter sets in."

After pondering some time over these enigmatical words, I said: "I daresay we are at cross purposes again. I mean," I added hurriedly, seeing the enquiring look on his face, "that we do not exactly understand each other, for the subject of honey was not in my thoughts."

"What, then, do you mean by a city?" he asked.

"What do I mean? Why, a city, I take it, is nothing more than a collection or congeries of houses—hundreds and thousands, or hundreds *of* thousands of houses, all built close together, where one can live very comfortably for years without seeing a blade of grass."

"I am afraid," he returned, "that the accident you met with in the mountains must have caused some injury to your brain; for I cannot in any other way account for these strange fantasies."

"Do you mean seriously to tell me, sir, that you have never even heard of the existence of a city, where millions of human beings live crowded together in a small space? Of course I mean a small space comparatively; for in some cities you might walk all day without getting into the fields; and a city like that might be compared to a bee-hive so large that a bee might fly in a straight line all day without getting out of it."

It struck me the moment I finished speaking that this comparison was not quite right somehow; but he did not ask me to explain: he had evidently ceased to pay any attention to what I said. The girl looked at me with an expression of pity, not to say contempt, and I felt at the same time ashamed and vexed. This served to rouse a kind of dogged spirit in me, and I returned to the subject once more.

"Surely," I said, "you have heard of such cities as Paris, Vienna, Rome, Athens, Babylon, Jerusalem?"

He only shook his head, and walked on in silence.

"And London! London is the capital of England. Why," I exclaimed, beginning to see light, and wondering at myself for not having seen it sooner, "you are at present talking to me in the English language."

"I fail to understand your meaning, and am even inclined to doubt that you have any," said he, a little ruffled. "I am addressing you in the language of human beings—that is all."

"Well, it seems awfully puzzling," said I; "but I hope you don't think I have been indulging in—well, tarradiddles." Then, seeing that I was making matters no clearer, I added: "I mean that I have not been telling untruths."

"I could not think that," he answered sternly. "It would indeed be a clouded mind which could mistake mere disordered fancies for wilful offences against the truth. I have no doubt that when you have recovered from the effects of your late accident these vain thoughts and imaginations will cease to trouble you."

"And in the meantime, perhaps, I had better say as little as possible," said I, with considerable temper. "At present we do not seem able to understand each other at all."

"You are right, we do not," he said; and then added with a grave smile, "although I must allow that this last remark of yours is quite intelligible."

"I'm glad of that," I returned. "It is distressing to talk and not be understood; it is like men calling to each other in a high wind, hearing voices but not able to distinguish words."

"Again I understand you," said he approvingly; while the beautiful girl bestowed on me the coveted reward of a smile, which had no pity or contempt in it.

"I think," I continued, determined to follow up this new train of ideas on which I had so luckily stumbled, "that we are not so far apart in mind after all. About some things we stand quite away from each other, like the widely diverging branches of a tree; but, like the branches, we have a meeting-place, and this is, I fancy, in that part of our nature where our feelings are. My accident in the hills has not disarranged that part of me, I am sure, and I can give you an instance. A little while ago when I was standing behind the bushes watching you all, I saw this young lady——"

Here a look of surprise and inquiry from the girl warned me that I was once more plunging into obscurity.

"When I saw *you,*" I continued, somewhat amused at her manner, "cast yourself on the earth to kiss the cold face of one you had loved in life, I felt the tears of sympathy come to my own eyes."

"Oh, how strange!" she exclaimed, flashing on me a glance from her green, mysterious eyes; and then, to increase my wonder and delight, she deliberately placed her hand in mine.

"And yet not strange," said the old man, by way of comment on her words.

"It seemed strange to Yoletta that one so unlike us outwardly should be so like us in heart," remarked the young man at her side.

There was something about this speech which I did not altogether like, though I could not detect anything like sarcasm in the tone of the speaker.

"And yet," continued the lovely girl, "you never saw him living—never heard his sweet voice, which still seems to come back to me like a melody from the distance."

"Was he your father?" I asked.

The question seemed to surprise her very much. "*He* is our father," she returned, with a glance at the old gentleman, which seemed strange, for he certainly looked aged enough to be her great-grandfather.

He smiled and said: "You forget, my daughter, that I am as little known to this stranger to our country as all the great and illustrious personages he has mentioned are to us."

At this point I began to lose interest in the conversation. It was enough for me to feel that I held that precious hand in mine, and presently I felt tempted to administer a gentle squeeze. She looked at me and smiled, then glanced over my whole person, the survey finishing at my boots, which seemed to have a disagreeable fascination for her. She shivered slightly, and withdrew her hand from mine, and in my heart I cursed those rusty, thick-soled monstrosities in which my feet were cased. However, we were all on a better footing now; and I resolved for the future to avoid all dangerous topics, historical and geographical, and confine myself to subjects relating to the emotional side of our natures.

At the end our way to the house was over a green turf, among great trees as in a park; and as there was no road or path, the first sight of the building seen near, when we emerged from the trees, came as a surprise. There were no gardens, lawns, enclosures or hedges near it, nor cultivation of any kind. It was like a wilderness, and the house produced the effect of a noble ruin. It was a hilly stone country where masses of stone cropped out here and there among the woods and on the green slopes, and it appeared that the house had been raised on the natural foundation of one of these rocks standing a little above the river that flowed behind it. The stone was grey, tinged with red, and the whole rock, covering an acre or so of ground, had been worn or hewn down to form a vast platform which stood about a dozen feet above the surrounding green level. The sloping and buttressed sides of the platform were clothed with ivy, wild shrubs, and various flowering plants. Broad, shallow steps led up to the house, which was all of the same material—reddish-grey stone; and the main entrance was beneath a lofty portico, the sculptured entablature of which was supported by sixteen huge caryatides, standing on round massive pedestals. The building was not high as a castle or cathedral; it was a dwelling-place, and had but one floor, and resembled a ruin to my eyes because of the extreme antiquity of its appearance, the weather-worn condition and massiness of the sculptured surfaces, and the masses of ancient ivy covering it in places. On the central portion of the building rested a great dome-shaped roof, resembling ground glass of a pale reddish tint, producing the effect of a cloud resting on the stony summit of a hill.

I remained standing on the grass about thirty yards from the first steps after the others had gone in, all but the old gentleman, who still kept with me. By-and-by, withdrawing to a stone bench under an oak-tree, he motioned to me to take a seat by his side. He said nothing, but appeared to be quietly enjoying my undisguised surprise and admiration.

"A noble mansion!" I remarked at length to my venerable host, feeling, Englishman-like, a sudden great access of respect towards the owner of a big house. Men in such a position can afford to be as eccentric as they like, even to the wearing of carnivalesque garments, burying their friends or relations in a park, and shaking their heads over such names as Smith or Shakespeare. "A glorious place! It must have cost a pot of money, and taken a long time to build."

"What you mean by a *pot of money* I do not know," said he. "When you add *a long time to build*, I am also puzzled to understand you. For are not all houses, like the forest of trees, the human race, the world we live in, eternal?"

"If they stand for ever they are so in one sense, I suppose," I answered, beginning to fear that I had already unfortunately broken the rule I had so recently laid down for my own guidance. "But the trees of the forest, to which you compare a house, spring from seed, do they not? and so have a beginning. Their end also, like the end of man, is to die and return to the dust."

"That is true," he returned; "it is, moreover, a truth which I do not now hear for the first time; but it has no connection with the subject we are discussing. Men pass away, and others take their places. Trees also decay, but the forest does not die, or suffer for the loss of individual trees; is it not the same with the house and the family inhabiting it, which is one with the house, and endures for ever, albeit the members composing it must all in time return to the dust?"

"Is there no decay, then, of the materials composing a house?"

"Assuredly there is! Even the hardest stone is worn in time by the elements, or by the footsteps of many generations of men; but the stone that decays is removed, and the house does not suffer."

"I have never looked at it quite in this light before," said I. "But surely we can build a house whenever we wish!"

"Build a house whenever we wish!" he repeated, with that astonished look which threatened to become the permanent expression of his face—so long as he had me to talk with, at any rate.

"Yes, or pull one down if we find it unsuitable——" But his look of horror here made me pause, and to finish the sentence I added: "Of course, you must admit that a house had a beginning?"

"Yes; and so had the forest, the mountain, the human race, the world itself. But the origin of all these things is covered with the mists of time."

"Does it never happen, then, that a house, however substantially built——"

"However what! But never mind; you continue to speak in riddles. Pray, finish what you were saying."

"Does it never happen that a house is overthrown by some

natural force—by floods, or subsidence of the earth, or is destroyed by lightning or fire?"

"No!" he answered, with such tremendous emphasis that he almost made me jump from my seat. "Are you alone so ignorant of these things that you speak of building and of pulling down a house?"

"Well, I fancied I knew a lot of things once," I answered, with a sigh. "But perhaps I was mistaken—people often are. I should like to hear you say something more about all these things—I mean about the house and the family, and the rest of it."

"Are you not, then, able to read—have you been taught absolutely nothing?"

"Oh yes, certainly I can read," I answered, joyfully seizing at once on the suggestion, which seemed to open a simple, pleasant way of escape from the difficulty. I am by no means a studious person; perhaps I am never so happy as when I have nothing to read. Nevertheless, I do occasionally look into books, and greatly appreciate their gentle, kindly ways. They never shut themselves up with a sound like a slap, or throw themselves at your head for a duffer, but seem silently grateful for being read, even by a stupid person, and teach you very patiently, like a pretty, meek-spirited young girl.

"I am very pleased to hear it," said he. "You shall read and learn all these things for yourself, which is the best method. Or perhaps I ought rather to say, you shall by reading recall them to your mind, for it is impossible to believe that it has always been in its present pitiable condition. I can only attribute such a mental state, with its disordered fancies about cities, or immense hives of human beings, and other things equally frightful to contemplate, and its absolute vacancy concerning ordinary matters of knowledge, to the grave accident you met with in the hills. Doubtless in falling your head was struck and injured by a stone. Let us hope that you will soon recover possession of your memory and other faculties. And now let us repair to the eating-room, for it is best to refresh the body first, and the mind afterwards."

III

WE ascended the steps, and passing through the portico went into the hall by what seemed to me a doorless way. It was not really so, as I discovered later; the doors, of which there were several, some of coloured glass, others of some other material, were simply thrust back into receptacles within the wall itself, which was five or six feet thick. The hall was the noblest I had ever seen; it had a stone and bronze fireplace some twenty or thirty feet long on one side, and several tall arched doorways on the other. The spaces between the doors were covered with sculpture, its material being a blue-grey stone combined or inlaid with a yellow metal, the effect being indescribably rich. The floor was mosaic of many dark colours, but with no definite pattern, and the concave roof was deep red in colour. Though beautiful, it was somewhat sombre, as the light was not strong. At all events, that is how it struck me at first on coming in from the bright sunlight. Nor, it appeared, was I alone in experiencing such a feeling. As soon as we were inside, the old gentleman, removing his cap and passing his thin fingers through his white hair, looked around him, and addressing some of the others, who were bringing in small round tables and placing them about the hall, said: "No, no; let us sup this evening where we can look at the sky."

The tables were immediately taken away.

Now some of those who were in the hall or who came in with the tables had not attended the funeral, and these were all astonished on seeing me. They did not stare at me, but I, of course, saw the expression on their faces, and noticed that the others who had made my acquaintance at the grave-side whispered in their ears to explain my presence. This made me extremely uncomfortable, and it was a relief when they began to go out again.

One of the men was seated near me; he was of those who had assisted in carrying the corpse, and he now turned to me and remarked: "You have been a long time in the open air, and probably feel the change as much as we do."

I assented, and he rose and walked away to the far end of the hall, where a great door stood facing the one by which we had entered. From the spot where I was—a distance of forty or fifty feet, perhaps—this door appeared to be of polished slate of a very dark grey, its surface ornamented with very large horse-chestnut leaves of brass or copper, or both, for they varied in shade from bright yellow to deepest copper-red. It was a double door with agate handles, and, first pressing on one handle, then on the other, he thrust it back into the walls on either side, revealing a new thing of beauty to my eyes, for behind the vanished door was a window, the sight of which came suddenly before me like a celestial vision. Sunshine, wind, cloud and rain had evidently inspired the artist who designed it, but I did not at the time understand the meaning of the symbolic figures appearing in the picture. Below, with loosened dark golden-red hair and amber-coloured garments fluttering in the wind, stood a graceful female figure on the summit of a grey rock; over the rock, and as high as her knees, slanted the thin branches of some mountain shrub, the strong wind even now stripping them of their remaining yellow and russet leaves, whirling them aloft and away. Round the woman's head was a garland of ivy leaves, and she was gazing aloft with expectant face, stretching up her arms, as if to implore or receive some precious gift from the sky. Above, against the slaty-grey cloud-rack, four exquisite slender girl-forms appeared, with loose hair, silver-grey drapery and gauzy wings as of ephemeræ, flying in pursuit of the cloud. Each carried a quantity of flowers, shaped like lilies, in her dress, held up with the left hand; one carried red lilies, another yellow, the third violet, and the last blue; and the gauzy wings and drapery of each was also touched in places with the same hue as the flowers she carried. Looking back in their flight they were all with the disengaged hand throwing down lilies to the standing figure.

This lovely window gave a fresh charm to the whole apartment, while the sunlight falling through it served also to reveal other beauties which I had not observed. One that quickly drew and absorbed my attention was a piece of statuary on the floor at some distance from me, and going to it I stood for some time gazing on it in the greatest delight. It was a statue about one-third the size of life, of a young woman seated on a white bull with golden horns. She had a graceful figure and beautiful countenance; the face, arms and feet were alabaster, the flesh tinted, but with colours more delicate than in nature. On her arms were broad golden armlets, and the drapery, a long flowing robe, was blue, embroidered with yellow flowers. A stringed instrument rested on her knee, and she was represented playing and singing. The bull, with lowered horns, appeared walking; about his chest hung a garland of flowers mingled with ears of yellow corn, oak, ivy, and various other leaves, green and russet, and acorns and crimson berries. The garland and blue dress were made of malachite, *lapis lazuli*, and various precious stones.

"Aha, my fair Phœnician, I know you well!" thought I exultingly, "though I never saw you before with a harp in your hand. But were you not gathering flowers, O lovely daughter of Agenor, when that celestial animal, that masquerading god, put himself so cunningly in your way to be admired and caressed, until you unsuspiciously placed yourself on his back? That explains the garland. I shall have a word to say about this pretty thing to my learned and very superior host."

The statue stood on an octagonal pedestal of a highly polished slaty-grey stone, and on each of its eight faces was a picture in which one human figure appeared. Now, from gazing on the statue itself I fell to contemplating one of these pictures with a very keen interest, for the figure, I recognised, was a portrait of the beautiful girl Yoletta. The picture was a winter landscape. The earth was white, not with snow, but with hoar frost; the distant trees, clothed by the frozen moisture as if with a feathery foliage, looked misty against the whitey-blue wintry sky. In the foreground, on the pale frosted grass, stood the girl, in a dark maroon dress, with silver embroidery on the bosom, and a dark red cap on her head. Close to her drooped the slender terminal twigs of a tree, sparkling with rime and icicle, and on the twigs were several small snow-white birds, hopping and fluttering down towards her outstretched hand; while she gazed up at them with flushed cheeks, and lips parting with a bright, joyous smile.

Presently, while I stood admiring this most lovely work, the young man I have mentioned as having raised Yoletta from the ground at the grave came to my side and remarked, smiling: "You have noticed the resemblance."

"Yes, indeed," I returned; "she is painted to the life."

"This is not Yoletta's portrait," he replied, "though it is very like her;" and then, when I looked at him incredulously, he pointed to some letters under the picture, saying: "Do you not see the name and date?"

Finding that I could not read the words, I hazarded the remark that it was Yoletta's mother, perhaps.

"This portrait was painted four centuries ago," he said, with surprise in his accent; and then he turned aside, thinking me, perhaps, a rather dull and ignorant person.

I did not want him to go away with that impression, and remarked, pointing to the statue I have spoken of: "I fancy I know very well who that is—that is Europa."

"Europa? That is a name I never heard; I doubt that any one in the house ever bore it." Then, with a half-puzzled smile, he added: "How could you possibly know unless you were told? No, that is Mistrelde. It was formerly the custom of the house for the Mother to ride on a white bull at the harvest festival. Mistrelde was the last to observe it."

"Oh, I see," I returned lamely, though I didn't see at all. The indifferent way in which he spoke of *centuries* in connection with this brilliant and apparently fresh-painted picture rather took me aback.

Presently he condescended to say something more. Pointing to the marks or characters which I could not read, he said: "You have seen the name of Yoletta here, and that and the resemblance misled you. You must know that there has always been a Yoletta in this house. This was the daughter of Mistrelde, the Mother, who died young and left but eight children; and when this work was made their portraits were placed on the eight faces of the pedestal."

"Thanks for telling me," I said, wondering if it was all true, or only a fantastic romance.

He then motioned me to follow him, and we quitted that room where it had been decided that we were not to sup.

IV

WE came to a large portico-like place open on three sides to the air, the roof being supported by slender columns. We were now on the opposite side of the house and looked upon the river, which was not more than a couple of hundred yards from the terrace or platform on which it stood. The ground here sloped rapidly to the banks, and, like that in the front, was a wilderness with rock and patches of tall fern and thickets of thorn and bramble, with a few trees of great size. Nor was wild life wanting in this natural park; some deer were feeding near the bank, while on the water numbers of wild duck and other water-fowl were disporting themselves, splashing and flapping over the surface and uttering shrill cries.

The people of the house were already assembled, standing and sitting by the small tables. There was a lively hum of conversation, which ceased on my entrance; then those who were sitting stood up and the whole company fixed its eyes on me, which was rather disconcerting.

The old gentleman, standing in the midst of the people, now bent on me a long, scrutinising gaze; he appeared to be waiting for me to speak, and, finding that I remained silent, he finally addressed me with solemnity. "Smith," he said—and I did not like it—"the meeting with you to-day was to me and to all of us a very strange experience: I little thought that an even stranger one awaited me, that before you break bread in this house in which you have found shelter, I should have to remind you that you are now in a house."

"Yes, I know I am," I said, and then added: "I'm sure, sir, I appreciate your kindness in bringing me here."

He had perhaps expected something more or something entirely different from me, as he continued standing with his eyes fixed on me. Then with a sigh, and looking round him, he said in a dissatisfied tone: "My children, let us begin, and for the present put out of our minds this matter which has been troubling us."

He then motioned me to a seat at his own table, where I was pleased to have a place since the lovely Yoletta was also there.

I am not particular about what I eat, as with me good digestion waits on appetite, and so long as I get a bellyful—to use a good old English word—I am satisfied. On this particular occasion, with or without a pretty girl at the table, I could have consumed a haggis—that greatest abomination ever invented by flesh-eating barbarians—I was so desperately hungry. It was therefore a disappointment when nothing more substantial than a plate of whitey-green, crisp-looking stuff resembling endive, was placed before me by one of the picturesque handmaidens. It was cold and somewhat bitter to the taste, but hunger compelled me to eat it even to the last green leaf; then, when I began to wonder if it would be right to ask for more, to my great relief other more succulent dishes followed, composed of various vegetables. We also had some pleasant drinks, made, I suppose, from the juices of fruits, but the delicious alcoholic sting was not in them. We had fruits, too, of unfamiliar flavours, and a confection of crushed nuts and honey.

We sat at table—or tables—a long time, and the meal was enlivened with conversation; for all now appeared in a cheerful frame of mind, notwithstanding the melancholy event which had occupied them during the day. It was, in fact, a kind of supper, and the one great meal of the day; the only other meals being a breakfast, and at noon a crust of brown bread, a handful of dried fruit, and drink of milk.

At the conclusion of the repast, during which I had been too much occupied to take notice of everything that passed, I observed that a number of small birds had flown in, and were briskly hopping over the floor and tables, also perching quite fearlessly on the heads or shoulders of the company, and that they were being fed with the fragments. I took them to be sparrows and things of that kind, but they did not look altogether familiar to me. One little fellow, most lively in his motions, was remarkably like my old friend the robin, only the bosom was more vivid, running almost into orange, and the wings and tail were tipped with the same hue, giving it quite a distinguished appearance. Another small olive-green bird, which I at first took for a green linnet, was even prettier, the throat and bosom being of a most delicate buff, crossed with a belt of velvet black. The bird that really seemed most like a common sparrow was chestnut, with a white throat and mouse-coloured wings and tail. These pretty little pensioners systematically avoided my neighbourhood, although I tempted them with crumbs and fruit; only one flew on to my table, but had no sooner done so than it darted away again, and out of the room, as if greatly alarmed. I caught the pretty girl's eye just then, and having finished eating, and being anxious to join the conversation, for I hate to sit silent when others are talking, I remarked that it was strange the little birds so persistently avoided me.

"Oh no, not at all strange," she replied, with surprising readiness, showing that she too had noticed it. "They are frightened at your appearance."

"I must indeed appear strange to them," said I, with some bitterness, and recalling the adventures of the morning. "It is to me a new and very painful experience to walk about the world frightening men, cattle, and birds; yet I suppose it is entirely due to the clothes I am wearing—and the boots. I wish some kind person would suggest a remedy for this state of things; for just now my greatest desire is to be dressed in accordance with the fashion."

"Allow me to interrupt you for one moment, Smith," said the old gentleman, who had been listening attentively to my words. "We understood what you said so well on this occasion that it seems a pity you should suddenly render yourself unintelligible. Can you explain to us what you mean by dressing in accordance with the fashion?"

"My meaning is, that I simply desire to dress like one of yourselves, to see the last of these *uncouth* garments." I could not help putting a little vicious emphasis on that hateful word.

He inclined his head and said, "Yes?"

Thus encouraged, I dashed boldly into the middle of the matter; for now, having dined, albeit without wine, I was inflamed with an intense craving to see myself arrayed in their rich, mysterious dress. "This being so," I continued, "may I ask you if it is in your power to provide me with the necessary garments, so that I may cease to be an object of aversion and offence to every living thing and person, myself included?"

A long and uncomfortable silence ensued, which was perhaps not strange, considering the nature of the request. That I had blundered once more seemed likely enough, from the general suspense and the somewhat alarmed expression of the old gentleman's countenance; nevertheless, my motives had been good: I had expressed my wish in that way for the sake of peace and quietness, and fearing that if I had asked to be directed to the nearest clothing establishment, a new fit of amazement would have been the result.

Finding the silence intolerable, I at length ventured to remark that I feared he had not understood me to the end.

"Perhaps not," he answered gravely. "Or, rather let me say, I hope not."

"May I explain my meaning?" said I, greatly distressed.

"Assuredly you may," he replied with dignity. "Only before you speak, let me put this plain question to you: Do you ask us to provide you with garments—that is to say, to bestow them as a gift on you?"

"Certainly not!" I exclaimed, turning crimson with shame to think that they were all taking me for a beggar. "My wish is to obtain them somehow from somebody, since I cannot make them for myself, and to give in return their full value."

I had no sooner spoken than I greatly feared that I had made matters worse; for here was I, a guest in the house, actually offering to purchase clothing—ready-made or to order—from my host, who, for all I knew, might be one of the aristocracy of the country. My fears, however, proved quite groundless.

"I am glad to hear your explanation," he answered, "for it has completely removed the unpleasant impression caused by your former words. What can you do in return for the garments you are anxious to possess? And here, let me remark, I approve highly of your wish to escape, with the least possible delay, from your present covering. Do you wish to confine yourself to the finishing of some work in a particular line—as wood-carving, or stone, metal, clay or glass work; or in making or using colours? or have you only that general knowledge of the various arts which would enable you to assist the more skilled in preparing materials?"

"No, I am not an artist," I replied, surprised at his question. "All I can do is to buy the clothes—to pay for them in money."

"What do you mean by that? What is money?"

"Surely——" I began, but fortunately checked myself in time, for I had meant to suggest that he was pulling my leg. But it was really hard to believe that a person of his years did not know what money was. Besides, I could not answer the question, having always abhorred the study of political economy, which tells you all about it; so that I had never learned to define money, but only how to spend it. Presently I thought the best way out of the muddle was to show him some, and I accordingly pulled out my big leather book-purse from my breast pocket. It had an ancient, musty smell, like everything else about me, but seemed pretty heavy and well filled, and I proceeded to open it and turn the contents on the table. Eleven bright sovereigns and three half-crowns or florins, I forget which, rolled out; then, unfolding the papers, I discovered three five-pound Bank of England notes.

"Surely this is very little for me to have about me!" said I, feeling greatly disappointed. "I fancy I must have been making ducks and drakes of a lot of cash before—before—well, before I was—I don't know what, or when, or where."

Little notice was taken of this somewhat incoherent speech, for all were now gathering round the table, examining the gold and notes with eager curiosity. At length the old gentleman, pointing to the gold pieces, said, "What are these?"

"Sovereigns," I answered, not a little amused. "Have you never seen any like them before?"

"Never. Let me examine them again. Yes, these eleven are of gold. They are all marked alike, on one side with a roughly-executed figure of a woman's head, with the hair gathered on its summit in a kind of ball. There are also other things on them which I do not understand."

"Can you not read the letters?" I asked.

"No. The letters—if these marks are letters—are incomprehensible to me. But what have these small pieces of metal to do with the question of your garments? You puzzle me."

"Why, everything. These pieces of metal, as you call them, are money, and represent, of course, so much buying power. I don't know yet what your currency is, and whether you have the dollar or the rupee"—here I paused, seeing that he did not follow me. "My idea is this," I resumed, and coming down to very plain speaking: "I can give one of these five-pound notes, or its equivalent in gold, if you prefer that—five of these sovereigns, I mean—for a suit of clothes such as you all wear."

So great was my desire to possess the clothes that I was about to double the offer, which struck me as poor, and add that I would give ten sovereigns; but when I had spoken he dropped the piece he held in his hand upon the table, and stared fixedly at me, assisted by all the others. Presently, in the profound silence which ensued, a low, silvery gurgling became audible, as of some merry mountain burn—a sweet, warbling sound, swelling louder by degrees until it ended in a loud ringing peal of laughter.

This was from the girl Yoletta. I stared at her, surprised at her unseasonable levity; but the only effect of my doing so was a general explosion, men and women joining in such a tempest of merriment that one might have imagined they had just heard the most wonderful joke ever invented since man acquired the sense of the ludicrous.

The old gentleman was the first to recover a decent gravity, although it was plain to see that he struggled severely at intervals to prevent a relapse.

"Smith," said he, "of all the extraordinary delusions you appear to be suffering from, this, that you can have garments to wear in return for a small piece of paper, or for a few bits of this metal, is the most astounding! You cannot exchange these trifles for clothes, because clothes are the fruit of much labour of many hands."

"And yet, sir, you said you understood me when I proposed to pay for the things I require," said I, in an aggrieved tone. "You seemed even to approve of the offer I made. How, then, am I to pay for them if all I possess is not considered of any value?"

"*All* you possess!" he replied. "Surely I did not say that! Surely you possess the strength and skill common to all men, and can acquire anything you wish by the labour of your hands."

I began once more to see light, although my skill, I knew, would not count for much. "Ah yes," I answered: "to go back to that subject, I do not know anything about wood-carving or using colours, but I might be able to do something—some work of a simpler kind."

"There are trees to be felled, land to be ploughed, and many other things to be done. If you will do these things some one else will be released to perform works of skill; and as these are the most agreeable to the worker, it would please us more to have you labour in the fields than in the workhouse."

"I am strong," I answered, "and will gladly undertake labour of the kind you speak of. There is, however, one difficulty. My desire is to change these clothes for others which will be more pleasing to the eye, at once; but the work I shall have to do in return will not be finished in a day. Perhaps not in—well, several days."

"No, of course not," said he. "A year's labour will be necessary to pay for the garments you require."

This staggered me; for if the clothes were given to me at the beginning, then before the end of the year they would be worn to rags, and I should make myself a slave for life. I was sorely perplexed in mind, and pulled about this way and that by the fear of incurring a debt, and the desire to see myself (and to be seen by Yoletta) in those strangely fascinating garments. That I had a decent figure, and was not a bad-looking young fellow, I was pretty sure; and the hope that I should be able to create an impression (favourable, I mean) on the heart of that supremely beautiful girl was very strong in me. At all events, by closing with the offer I should have a year of happiness in her society, and a year of healthy work in the fields could not hurt me, or interfere much with my prospects. Besides, I was not quite sure that my prospects were really worth thinking about just now. Certainly, I had always lived comfortably, spending money, eating and drinking of the best, and dressing well—that is, according to the London standard. And there was my dear old bachelor Uncle Jack—John Smith, Member of Parliament for Wormwood Scrubbs. That is to say, ex-Member; for, being a Liberal when the great change came at the last general election, he was ignominiously ousted from his seat, the Scrubbs proving at the finish a bitter place to him. He was put out in more ways than one, and tried to comfort himself by saying that there would soon be another dissolution—thinking of his own, possibly, being an old man. I remembered that I had rather looked forward to such a contingency, thinking how pleasant it would be to have all that money, and cruise about the world in my own yacht, enjoying myself as I knew how. And really I had some reason to hope. I remember he used to wind up the talk of an evening when I dined with him (and got a cheque) by saying: "My boy, you have talents, if you'd only use 'em." Where were those talents now? Certainly they had not made me shine much during the last few hours.

Now, all this seemed unsubstantial, and I remembered these things dimly, like a dream or a story told to me in childhood; and sometimes, when recalling the past, I seemed to be thinking about ancient history—Sesostris, and the Babylonians and Assyrians, and that sort of thing. And, besides, it would be very hard to get back from a place where even the name of London was unknown. And perhaps, if I ever should succeed in getting back, it would only be to encounter a second Roger Tichborne case, or to be confronted with the statute of limitations. Anyhow, a year could not make much difference, and I should also keep my money, which seemed an advantage, though it wasn't much. I looked up: they were all once more studying the coins and notes, and exchanging remarks about them.

"If I bind myself to work one year," said I, "shall I have to wait until the end of that time before I get the clothes?"

The reply to this question, I thought, would settle the matter one way or the other.

"No," said he. "It is your wish, and also ours, that you should be differently clothed at once, and the garments you require would be made for you immediately."

"Then," said I, taking the desperate plunge, "I should like to have them as soon as possible, and I am ready to commence work at once."

"You shall commence to-morrow morning," he answered, smiling at my impetuosity. "The daughters of the house, whose province it is to make these things, shall also suspend other work until your garments are finished. And now, my son, from this evening you are one of the house and one of us, and the things which we possess you also possess in common with us."

I rose and thanked him. He too rose, and, after looking round on us with a fatherly smile, went away to the interior of the house.

V

WHEN he was gone, and Yoletta had followed, leaving some of the others still studying those wretched sovereigns, I sat down again and rested my chin on my hand; for I was now thinking—deeply: thinking on the terms of the agreement. "I daresay I have succeeded in making a precious ass of myself," was the mental reflection that occurred to me—one I had not infrequently made, and, what is more, been justified in making on former occasions. Then, remembering that I had come to supper with an extravagant appetite, it struck me that my host, quietly observant, had, when proposing terms, taken into account the quantity of food necessary for my sustenance. I regretted too late that I had not exercised more restraint; but the hungry man does not and cannot consider consequences, else a certain hairy gentleman who figures in ancient history had never lent himself to that nefarious compact, which gave so great an advantage to a younger but sleek and well-nourished brother. In spite of all this, I felt a secret satisfaction in the thought of the clothes, and it was also good to know that the nature of the work I had undertaken would not lower my status in the house.

Occupied with these reflections, I had failed to observe that the company had gradually been drifting away until but one person was left with me—the young man who had talked with me before. On his invitation I now rose, put by my money, and followed him. Returning by the hall we went through a passage and entered a room of vast extent, which in its form and great length and high arched roof was like the nave of a cathedral. And yet how unlike in that something ethereal in its aspect, as of a nave in a cloud cathedral, its far-stretching shining floors and walls and columns, pure white and pearl-grey, faintly touched with colours of exquisite delicacy. And over it all was the roof of white or pale grey glass tinged with golden-red—the roof which I had seen from the outside when it seemed to me like a cloud resting on the stony summit of a hill.

On coming in I had the impression of an empty, silent place; yet the inmates of the house were all there; they were sitting and reclining on low couches, some lying at their ease on straw mats on the floor; some were reading, others were occupied with some work in their hands, and some were conversing, the sound coming to me like a faint murmur from a distance.

At one side, somewhere about the centre of the room, there was a broad raised place, or daïs, with a couch on it, on which the father was reclining at his ease. Beside the couch stood a lectern on which a large volume rested, and before him there was a brass box or cabinet, and behind the couch seven polished brass globes were ranged, suspended on axles resting on bronze frames. These globes varied in size, the largest being not less than about twelve feet in circumference.

I noticed that there were books on a low stand near me. They were all folios, very much alike in form and thickness; and seeing presently that the others were all following their own inclinations, and considering that I had been left to my own resources and that it is a good plan when at Rome to do as the Romans do, I by-and-by ventured to help myself to a volume, which I carried to one of the reading-stands.

Books are grand things—sometimes, thought I, prepared to follow the advice I had received, and find out by reading all about the customs of this people, especially their ideas concerning *The House*, which appeared to be an object of almost religious regard with them. This would make me quite independent, and teach me how to avoid blundering in the future, or giving expression to any more "extraordinary delusions." On opening the volume I was greatly surprised to find that it was richly illuminated on every leaf, the middle only of each page being occupied with a rather narrow strip of writing; but the minute letters, resembling Hebrew characters, were incomprehensible to me. I bore the disappointment very cheerfully, I must say, for I am not over-fond of study; and, besides, I could not have paid proper attention to the text, surrounded with all that distracting beauty of graceful design and brilliant colouring.

After a while Yoletta came slowly across the room, her fingers engaged with some kind of wool-work as she walked, and my heart beat fast when she paused by my side.

"You are not reading," she said, looking curiously at me. "I have been watching you for some time."

"Have you indeed?" said I, not knowing whether to feel flattered or not. "No, unfortunately, I can't read this book, as I do not understand the letters. But what a wonderfully beautiful book it is! I was just thinking what some of the great London book-buyers—Quaritch, for instance—would be tempted to give for it. Oh, I am forgetting—you have never heard his name, of course; but—but what a beautiful book it is!"

She said nothing in reply, and only looked a little surprised—disgusted, I feared—at my ignorance, then walked away. I had hoped that she was going to talk to me, and with keen disappointment watched her moving across the floor. All the glory seemed now to have gone out of the leaves of the volume, and I continued turning them over listlessly, glancing at intervals at the beautiful girl, who was also like one of the pages before me, wonderful to look at and hard to understand. In a distant part of the room I saw her place some cushions on the floor, and settle herself on them to do her work.

The sun had set by this time, and the interior was growing darker by degrees; the fading light, however, seemed to make no difference to those who worked or read. They appeared to be gifted with an owlish vision, able to see with very little light. The father alone did nothing, but still rested on his couch, perhaps indulging in a post-prandial nap. At length he roused himself and looked around him.

"There is no melody in our hearts this evening, my children," he said. "When another day has passed over us it will perhaps be different. To-night the voice so recently stilled in death for ever would be too painfully missed by all of us."

Some one then rose and brought a tall wax taper and placed it near him. The flame threw a little brightness on the volume, which he now proceeded to open; and here and there, further away, it flashed and trembled in points of rainbow-coloured light on a tall column; but the greater part of the room still remained in twilight obscurity.

He began to read aloud, and, although he did not seem to raise his voice above its usual pitch, the words he uttered fell on my ears with a distinctness and purity of sound which made them seem like a melody "sweetly played in tune." The words he read related to life and death, and such solemn matters; but to my mind his theology seemed somewhat fantastical, although it is right to confess that I am no judge of such matters. There was also a great deal about the *house*, which did not enlighten me much, being too rhapsodical, and when he spoke about our conduct and aims in life, and things of that kind, I understood him little better. Here is a part of his discourse:—

"It is natural to grieve for those that die, because light and knowledge and love and joy are no longer theirs; but they grieve not any more, being now asleep on the lap of the Universal Mother, the bride of the Father, who is with us, sharing our sorrow, which was his first; but it dims not his everlasting brightness; and his desire and our glory is that we should always and in all things resemble him.

"The end of every day is darkness, but the Father of life through our reason has taught us to mitigate the exceeding bitterness of our end; otherwise, we that are above all other creatures in the earth should have been at the last more miserable than they. For in the irrational world, between the different kinds, there reigns perpetual strife and bloodshed, the strong devouring the weak and the incapable; and when failure of life clouds the brightness of that lower soul, which is theirs, the end is not long delayed. Thus the life that has lasted many days goes out with a brief pang, and in its going gives new vigour to the strong that have yet many days to live. Thus also does the ever-living earth from the dust of dead generations of leaves re-make a fresh foliage, and for herself a new garment.

"We only, of all things having life, being like the Father, slay not nor are slain, and are without enemies in the earth; for even the lower kinds, which have not reason, know without reason that we are highest on the earth, and see in us, alone of all his works, the majesty of the Father, and lose all their rage in our presence. Therefore, when the night is near, when life is a burden and we remember our mortality, we hasten the end, that those we love may cease to sorrow at the sight of our decline; and we know that this is his will who called us into being, and gave us life and joy on the earth for a season, but not for ever.

"It is bitter to lay down the life that is ours, to leave all things—the love of our kindred; the beauty of the world and of the house; the labour in which we take delight, to go forth and be no more: but the bitterness endures not, and is scarcely tasted when in our last moments we remember that our labour has borne fruit; that the letters we have written perish not with us, but remain as a testimony and a joy to succeeding generations, and live in the house for ever.

"For the house is the image of the world, and we that live and labour in it are the image of our Father who made the world; and, like him, we labour to make for ourselves a worthy habitation, which shall not shame our teacher. This is his desire; for in all his works, and that knowledge which is like pure water to one that thirsts, and satisfies and leaves no taste of bitterness on the palate, we learn the will of him that called us into life. All the knowledge we seek, the invention and skill we possess, and the labour of our hands, has this purpose only: for all knowledge and invention and labour having any other purpose whatsoever is empty and vain in comparison, and unworthy of those that are made in the image of the Father of life. For just as the bodily senses may become perverted, and the taste lose its discrimination, so that the hungry man will devour acrid fruits and poisonous herbs for aliment, so is the mind capable of seeking out new paths, and a knowledge which leads only to misery and destruction.

"Thus we know that in the past men sought after knowledge of various kinds, asking not whether it was for good or for evil: but every offence of the mind and the body has its appropriate reward; and while their knowledge grew apace, that better knowledge and discrimination which the Father gives to every living soul, both in man and in beast, was taken from them. Thus by increasing their riches they were made poorer; and, like one who, forgetting the limits that are set to his faculties, gazes steadfastly on the sun, by seeing much they become afflicted with blindness. But they knew not their poverty and blindness, and were not satisfied; but were like shipwrecked men on a lonely and barren rock in the midst of the sea, who are consumed with thirst, and drink of no sweet spring, but of the bitter wave, and thirst, and drink again, until madness possesses their brains, and death releases them from their misery. Thus did they thirst, and drink again, and were crazed; being inflamed with the desire to learn the secrets of nature, hesitating not to dip their hands in blood, seeking in the living tissues of animals for the hidden springs of life. For in their madness they hoped by knowledge to gain absolute dominion over nature, thereby taking from the Father of the world his prerogative.

"But their vain ambition lasted not, and the end of it was death. The madness of their minds preyed on their bodies, and worms were bred in their corrupted flesh: and these, after feeding on their tissues, changed their forms; and becoming winged, flew out in the breath of their nostrils, like clouds of winged ants that issue in the spring-time from their breeding-places; and, flying from body to body, filled the race of men in all places with corruption and decay; and the Mother of men was thus avenged of her children for their pride and folly, for they perished miserably, devoured of worms.

"Of the human race only a small remnant survived, these being men of an humble mind, who had lived apart and unknown to their fellows; and after long centuries they went forth into the wilderness of earth and re-peopled it: but nowhere did they find any trace or record of those that had passed away; for earth had covered all their ruined works with her dark mould and green forests, even as a man hides unsightly scars on his body with a new and beautiful garment. Nor is it known to us when this destruction fell upon the race of men; we only know that the history thereof was graven an hundred centuries ago on the granite pillars of the House of Evor, on the plains between the sea and the snow-covered mountains of Elf. Thither in past ages some of our pilgrims journeyed, and have brought a record of these things; nor in our house only are they known, but in many houses throughout the world have they been written for the instruction of all men and a warning for all time.

"But to mankind there shall come no second darkness of error, nor seeking after vain knowledge; and in the Father's House there shall be no second desolation, but the sounds of joy and melody, which were silent, shall be heard everlastingly; since we had now continued long in this even mind, seeking only to inform ourselves of his will; until as in a clear crystal without flaw shining with coloured light, or as a glassy lake reflecting within itself the heavens and every cloud and star, so is he reflected in our minds; and in the house we are his vicegerents, and in the world his co-workers; and for the glory which he has in his work we have a like glory in ours.

"He is our teacher. Morning and evening throughout the various world, in the procession of the seasons, and in the blue heavens powdered with stars; in mountain and plain and many-toned forest; in the sounding walls of the ocean, and in the billowy seas through which we pass in peril from land to land, we read his thoughts and listen to his voice. Here do we learn with what far-seeing intelligence he has laid the foundations of his everlasting mansion, how skilfully he has builded its walls, and with what prodigal richness he has decorated all his works. For the sunlight and moonlight and the blueness of heaven are his; the sea with its tides; the blackness and the lightnings of the tempest, and snow, and changeful winds, and green and yellow leaf; his are also the silver rain and the rainbow, the shadows and the many-coloured mists, which he flings like a mantle over all the world. Herein do we learn that he loves a stable building, and that the foundations and walls shall endure for ever: yet loves not sameness; thus, from day to day and from season to season do all things change their aspect, and the walls and floor and roof of his dwelling are covered with a new glory. But to us it is not given to rise to this supreme majesty in our works; therefore do we, like him yet unable to reach so great a height, borrow nothing one from the other, but in each house learn separately from him alone who has infinite riches; so that every habitation, changeless and eternal in itself, shall yet differ from all others, having its own special beauty and splendour: for we inhabit one house only, but the Father of men inhabits all.

"These things are written for the refreshment and delight of those who may no longer journey into distant lands; and they are in the library of the house in the seven thousand volumes of the Houses of the World which our pilgrims have visited in past ages. For once in a lifetime is it ordained that a man shall leave his own place and travel for the space of ten years, visiting the most famous houses in every land he enters, and also seeking out those of which no report has reached us.

"When the time for this chief adventure comes, and we go forth for a long period, there is compensation for every weariness, with absence of kindred and the sweet shelter of our own home: for now do we learn the infinite riches of the Father; for just as the day changes every hour, from the morning to the evening twilight, so does the aspect of the world alter as we progress from day to day; and in all places our fellow-men, learning as we do from him only, and seeing that which is nearest, give a special colour of nature to their lives and their houses; and every house, with the family which inhabits it, in their conversation and the arts in which they excel, is like a round lake set about with hills, wherein may be seen that visible world. And in all the earth there is no land without inhabitants, whether on wide continents or islands of the sea; and in all nature there is no grandeur or beauty or grace which men have not copied; knowing that this is pleasing to the Father: for we, that are made like him, delight not to work without witnesses; and we are his witnesses in the earth, taking pleasure in his works, even as he also does in ours.

"Thus, at the beginning of our journey to the far south, where we go to look first on those bright lands, which have hotter suns and a greater variety than ours, we come to the wilderness of Coradine, which seems barren and desolate to our sight, accustomed to the deep verdure of woods and valleys, and the blue mists of an abundant moisture. There a stony soil brings forth only thorns, and thistles, and sere tufts of grass; and blustering winds rush over the unsheltered reaches, where the rough-haired goats huddle for warmth; and there is no melody save the many-toned voices of the wind and the plover's wild cry. There dwell the children of Coradine, on the threshold of the wind-vexed wilderness, where the stupendous columns of green glass uphold the roof of the House of Coradine; the ocean's voice is in their rooms, and the inland-blowing wind brings to them the salt spray and yellow sand swept at low tide from the desolate floors of the sea, and the white-winged bird flying from the black tempest screams aloud in their shadowy halls. There, from the high terraces, when the moon is at its full, we see the children of Coradine gathered together, arrayed like no others, in shining garments of gossamer threads, when, like thistle-down chased by eddying winds, now whirling in a cloud, now scattering far apart, they dance their moonlight dances on the wide alabaster floors; and coming and going they pass away, and seem to melt into the moonlight, yet ever to return again with changeful melody and new measures. And, seeing this, all those things in which we ourselves excel seem poor in comparison, becoming pale in our memories. For the winds and waves, and the whiteness and grace, has been ever with them; and the winged seed of the thistle, and the flight of the gull, and the storm-vexed sea, flowering in foam, and the light of the moon on sea and barren land, have taught them this art, and a swiftness and grace which they alone possess.

"Yet does this moonlight dance, which is the chief glory of the House of Coradine, grow pale in the mind, and is speedily forgotten, when another is seen; and, going on our way from house to house, we learn how everywhere the various riches of the world have been taken into his soul by man, and made part of his life. Nor are we inferior to others, having also an art and chief excellence which is ours only, and the fame of which has long gone forth into the world; so that from many distant lands pilgrims gather yearly to our fields to listen to our harvest melody, when the sun-ripened fruits have been garnered, and our lips and hands make undying music, to gladden the hearts of those that hear it all their lives long. For then do we rejoice beyond others, rising like bright-winged insects from our lowly state to a higher life of glory and joy, which is ours for the space of three whole days. Then the august Mother, in a brazen chariot, is drawn from field to field by milk-white bulls with golden horns; then her children are gathered about her in shining yellow garments, with armlets of gold upon their arms; and with voice and instruments of forms unknown to the stranger, they make glad the listening fields with the great harvest melody.

"In ancient days the children of our house conceived it in their hearts, hearing it in all nature's voices; and it was with them day and night, and they whispered it to one another when it was no louder than the whisper of the wind in the forest leaves; and as the Builder of the world brings from an hundred far places the mist, and the dew, and the sunshine, and the light west wind, to give to the morning hour its freshness and glory; and as we, his humbler followers, seek far off in caverns of the hills and in the dark bowels of the earth for minerals and dyes that outshine the flowers and the sun, to beautify the walls of our house, so everywhere by night and day for long centuries did we listen to all sounds, and made their mystery and melody ours, until this great song was perfected in our hearts, and the fame of it in all lands has caused our house to be called the House of the Harvest Melody; and when the yearly pilgrims behold our procession in the fields, and listen to our song, all the glory of the world seems to pass before them, overcoming their hearts, until, bursting into tears and loud cries, they cast themselves upon the earth and worship the Father of the whole world.

"This shall be the chief glory of our house for ever; when a thousand years have gone by, and we that are now living, like those that have been, are mingled with the nature we come from, and speak to our children only in the wind's voice, and the cry of the passage-bird, pilgrims shall still come to these sun-bright fields, to rejoice, and worship the Father of the world, and bless the august Mother of the house, from whose sacred womb ever comes to it life and love and joy, and the harvest melody that shall endure for ever."

VI

THE reading went on, not of course "for ever," like that harvest melody he spoke of, but for a considerable time. The words, I concluded, were for the initiated, and not for me, and after a while I gave up trying to make out what it was all about. Those last expressions I have quoted about the "august Mother of the house" were unintelligible, and appeared to me meaningless. I had already come to the conclusion that however many of the ladies of the establishment might have experienced the pleasures and pains of maternity, there was really no mother of the house in the sense that there was a father of the house: that is to say, one possessing authority over the others and calling them all her children indiscriminately. Yet this mysterious non-existent mother of the house was continually being spoken of, as I found now and afterwards when I listened to the talk around me. After thinking the matter over, I came to the conclusion that "mother of the house" was merely a convenient fiction, and simply stood for the general sense of the women-folk, or something of the sort. It was perhaps stupid of me, but the story of Mistrelde, who died young, leaving *only* eight children, I had regarded as a mere legend or fable of antiquity.

To return to the reading. Just as I had been absorbed before in that beautiful book without being able to read it, so now I listened to that melodious and majestic voice, experiencing a singular pleasure without properly understanding the sense. I remembered now with a painful feeling of inferiority that my *thick* speech had been remarked on earlier in the day; and I could not but think that, compared with the speech of this people, it *was* thick. In their rare physical beauty, the colour of their eyes and hair, and in their fascinating dress, they had struck me as being utterly unlike any people ever seen by me. But it was perhaps in their clear, sweet, penetrative voice, which sometimes reminded me of a tender-toned wind instrument, that they most differed from others.

The reading, I have said, had struck me as almost of the nature of a religious service; nevertheless, everything went on as before—

reading, working, and occasional conversation; but the subdued talking and moving about did not interfere with one's pleasure in the old man's musical speech any more than the soft murmur and flying about of honey bees would prevent one from enjoying the singing of a skylark. Emboldened by what I saw the others doing, I left my seat and made my way across the floor to Yoletta's side, stealing through the gloom with great caution to avoid making a clatter with those abominable boots.

"May I sit down near you?" said I with some hesitation; but she encouraged me with a smile and placed a cushion for me.

I settled myself down in the most graceful position I could assume, which was not at all graceful, doubling my objectionable legs out of her sight; and then began my trouble, for I was greatly perplexed to know what to say to her. I thought of lawn-tennis and archery, Ellen Terry's acting, the Royal Academy Exhibition, private theatricals, and twenty things besides, but they all seemed unsuitable subjects to start conversation with in this case. There was, I began to fear, no common ground on which we could meet and exchange thoughts, or, at any rate, words. Then I remembered that ground, common and broad enough, of our human feelings, especially the sweet and important feeling of love. But how was I to lead up to it? The work she was engaged with at length suggested an opening, and the opportunity to make a pretty little speech.

"Your sight must be as good as your eyes are pretty," said I, "to enable you to work in such a dim light."

"Oh, the light is good enough," she answered, taking no notice of the compliment. "Besides, this is such easy work I could do it in the dark."

"It is very pretty work—may I look at it?"

She handed the stuff to me, but instead of taking it in the ordinary way, I placed my hand under hers, and, holding up cloth and hand together, proceeded to give a minute and prolonged scrutiny to her work.

"Do you know that I am enjoying two distinct pleasures at one and the same time?" said I. "One is in seeing your work, the other in holding your hand; and I think the last pleasure even greater than the first." As she made no reply, I added somewhat lamely: "May I—keep on holding it?"

"That would prevent me from working," she answered, with the utmost gravity. "But you may hold it for a little while."

"Oh, thank you," I exclaimed, delighted with the privilege; and then, to make the most of my precious "little while," I pressed it warmly, whereupon she cried out aloud: "Oh, Smith, you are squeezing too hard—you hurt my hand!"

I dropped it instantly in the greatest confusion. "Oh, for goodness sake," I stammered, "please, do not make such an outcry! You don't know what a hobble you'll get me into."

Fortunately, no notice was taken of the exclamation, though it was hard to believe that her words had not been overheard; and presently, recovering from my fright, I apologised for hurting her, and hoped she would forgive me.

"There is nothing to forgive," she returned gently. "You did not really squeeze hard, only my hand hurts, because to-day when I pressed it on the ground beside the grave I ran a small thorn into it." Then the remembrance of that scene at the burial brought a sudden mist of tears into her lovely eyes.

"I am so sorry I hurt you, Yoletta—may I call you Yoletta?" said I, all at once remembering that she had called me Smith, without the customary prefix.

"Why, that is my name—what else should you call me?" she returned, evidently with surprise.

"It is a pretty name, and so sweet on the lips that I should like to be repeating it continually," I answered. "But it is only right that you should have a pretty name, because—well, if I may tell you, because you are so very beautiful."

"Yes; but is that strange—are not all people beautiful?"

I thought of certain London types, especially among the "criminal classes," and of the old women with withered, simian faces and wearing shawls, slinking in or out of public-houses at the street corners; and also of some people of a better class I had known personally—some even in the House of Commons; and I felt that I could not agree with her, much as I wished to do so, without straining my conscience.

"At all events, you will allow," said I, evading the question, "that there are *degrees* of beauty, just as there are degrees of light. You may be able to see to work in this light, but it is very faint compared with the noonday light when the sun is shining."

"Oh, there is not so great a difference between people as *that*," she replied, with the air of a philosopher. "There are different kinds of beauty, I allow, and some people seem more beautiful to us than others, but that is only because we love them more. The best loved are always the most beautiful."

This seemed to reverse the usual idea, that the more beautiful the person is the more he or she gets loved. However, I was not going to disagree with her any more, and only said: "How sweetly you talk, Yoletta; you are as wise as you are beautiful. I could wish for no greater pleasure than to sit here listening to you the whole evening."

"Ah, then, I am sorry I must leave you now," she answered, with a bright smile which made me think that perhaps my little speech had pleased her.

"Do you wonder why I smile?" she added, as if able to read my thoughts. "It is because I have often heard words like yours from one who is waiting for me now."

This speech caused me a jealous pang. But for a few moments after speaking, she continued regarding me with that bright, spiritual smile on her lips; then it faded, and her face clouded and her glance fell. I did not ask her to tell me, nor did I ask myself, the reason of that change; and afterwards how often I noticed that same change in her, and in the others too—that sudden silence and clouding of the face, such as may be seen in one who freely expresses himself to a person who cannot hear, and then, all at once but too late, remembers the other's infirmity.

"Must you go?" I only said. "What shall I do alone?"

"Oh, you shall not be alone," she replied, and going away returned presently with another lady. "This is Edra," she said simply. "She will take my place by your side and talk with you."

I could not tell her that she had taken my words too literally, that being alone simply meant being separated from her; but there was no help for it, and some one, alas! some one I greatly hated was waiting for her. I could only thank her and her friend for their kind intentions. But what in the name of goodness was I to say to this beautiful woman who was sitting by me? She was certainly very beautiful, with a far more mature and perhaps a nobler beauty than Yoletta's, her age being about twenty-seven or twenty-eight; but the divine charm in the young girl's face could, for me, exist in no other.

Presently she opened the conversation by asking me if I disliked being alone.

"Well, no, perhaps not exactly that," I said; "but I think it much jollier—much more pleasant, I mean—to have some very nice person to talk to."

She assented, and, pleased at her ready intelligence, I added, "And it is particularly pleasant when you are understood. But I have no fear that you, at any rate, will fail to understand anything I may say."

"You have had some trouble to-day," she returned, with a charming smile. "I sometimes think that women can understand even more readily than men."

"There's not a doubt of it!" I returned warmly, glad to find that with Edra it was all plain sailing. "It must be patent to every one that women have far quicker finer intellects than men, although their brains are smaller; but then quality is more important than mere quantity. And yet," I continued, "some people hold that women ought not to have the franchise, or suffrage, or whatever it is! Not that I care two straws about the question myself, and I only hope they'll never get it; but then I think it is so illogical—don't you?"

"I am afraid I do not understand you, Smith," she returned, looking much distressed.

"Well, no, I suppose not, but what I said was of no consequence," I replied; then, wishing to make a fresh start, I added: "But I am so glad to hear you call me Smith. It makes it so much more pleasant and home-like to be treated without formality. It is very kind of you, I'm sure."

"But surely your name is Smith?" said she, looking very much surprised.

"Oh yes, my name is Smith: only of course—well, the fact is, I was just wondering what to call you."

"My name is Edra," she replied, looking more bewildered than ever; and from that moment the conversation, which had begun so favourably, was nothing but a series of entanglements, from which I could only escape in each case by breaking the threads of the subject under discussion, and introducing a new one.

VII

THE moment of retiring, to which I had been looking forward with considerable interest as one likely to bring fresh surprises, arrived at last: it brought only extreme discomfort. I was conducted (without a flat candlestick) along an obscure passage; then, at right angles with the first, a second broader, lighter passage, leading past a great many doors placed near together. These, I ascertained later, were the dormitories, or sleeping-cells, and were placed side by side in a row opening on the terrace at the back of the house. Having reached the door of my box, my conductor pushed back the sliding-panel, and when I had groped my way to the dark interior, closed it again behind me. There was no light for me except the light of the stars; for directly opposite the door by which I had entered stood another, open wide to the night, which was apparently not intended ever to be closed. The prospect was the one I had already seen—the wilderness sloping to the river, and the glassy surface of the broad water, reflecting the stars, and the black masses of large trees. There was no sound save the hooting of an owl in the distance, and the wailing note of some mournful-minded water-fowl. The night air blew in cold and moist, which made my bones ache, though they were not broken; and feeling very sleepy and miserable, I groped about until I was rewarded by discovering a narrow bed, or cot of trellis-work, on which was a hard straw pallet and a small straw pillow; also, folded small, a kind of woollen sleeping garment. Too tired to keep out of even such an uninviting bed, I flung off my clothes, and with my mouldy tweeds for only covering I laid me down, but not to sleep. The misery of it! for although my body was warm—too warm, in fact—the wind blew on my face and bare feet and legs, and made it impossible to sleep.

About midnight, I was just falling into a doze when a sound as of a person coming with a series of jumps into the room disturbed me; and starting up I was horrified to see, sitting on the floor, a great beast much too big for a dog, with large, erect ears. He was intently watching me, his round eyes shining like a pair of green phosphorescent globes. Having no weapon, I was at the brute's mercy, and was about to utter a loud shout to summon assistance, but as he sat so still I refrained, and began even to hope that he would go quietly away. Then he stood up, went back to the door and sniffed audibly at it; and thinking that he was about to relieve me of his unwelcome presence, I dropped my head on the pillow and lay perfectly still. Then he turned and glared at me again, and finally, advancing deliberately to my side, sniffed at my face. It was all over with me now, I thought, and closing my eyes, and feeling my forehead growing remarkably moist in spite of the cold, I murmured a little prayer. When I looked again the brute had vanished, to my inexpressible relief.

It seemed very astonishing that an animal like a wolf should come into the house; but I soon remembered that I had seen no dogs about, so that all kinds of savage, prowling beasts could come in with impunity. It was getting beyond a joke: but then all this seemed only a fit ending to the perfectly absurd arrangement into which I had been induced to enter. "Goodness gracious!" I exclaimed, sitting bolt upright on my straw bed, "am I a rational being or an inebriated donkey, or what, to have consented to such a proposal? It is clear that I was not quite in my right mind when I made the agreement, and I am therefore not morally bound to observe it. What! be a field labourer, a hewer of wood and drawer of water, and sleep on a miserable straw mat in an open porch, with wolves for visitors at all hours of the night, and all for a few barbarous rags! I don't know much about ploughing and that sort of thing, but I suppose any able-bodied man can earn a pound a week, and that would be fifty-two pounds for a suit of clothes. Who ever heard of such a thing! Wolves and all thrown in for nothing! I daresay I shall have a tiger dropping in presently just to have a look round. No, no, my venerable friend, that was all excellent acting about my extraordinary delusions, and the rest of it, but I am not going to be carried so far by them as to adhere to such an outrageously one-sided bargain."

Presently I remembered two things—divine Yoletta was the first; and the second was that thought of the rare pleasure it would be to array myself in those same "barbarous rags," as I had blasphemously called them. These things had entered into my soul, and had become a part of me—especially—well, both. Those strange garments had looked so refreshingly picturesque, and I had conceived such an intense longing to wear them! Was it a very contemptible ambition on my part? Is it sinful to wish for any adornments other than wisdom and sobriety, a meek and loving spirit, good works, and other things of the kind? Straight into my brain flashed the words of a sentence I had recently read—that is to say, just before my accident—in a biological work, and it comforted me as much as if an angel with shining face and rainbow-coloured wings had paid me a visit in my dusky cell: "*Unto Adam also, and his wife, did the Lord God make coats of skin and clothed them.* This has become, as every one knows, a custom among the race of men, and shows at present no sign of becoming obsolete. Moreover, that first correlation, namely, milk-glands and a hairy covering, appears to have entered the very soul of creatures of this class, and to have become *psychical* as well as *physical,* for in that type, which is only *for a while* inferior to the angels, the fondness for this kind of outer covering is a strong, ineradicable passion!" Most true and noble words, O biologist of the fiery soul! It was a delight to remember them. A "strong and ineradicable passion," not merely to clothe the body, but to clothe it appropriately, that is to say, beautifully, and by so doing please God and ourselves. This being so, must we go on for ever scraping our faces with a sharp iron, until they are blue and spotty with manifold scrapings; and cropping our hair short to give ourselves an artificial resemblance to old dogs and monkeys—creatures lower than us in the scale of being—and array our bodies, like mutes at a funeral, in repulsive black—we, "Eutheria of the Eutheria, the noble of the noble?" And all for what, since it pleases not heaven nor accords with our own desires? For the sake of respectability, perhaps, whatever that may mean. Oh, then, a million curses take it—respectability, I mean; may it sink into the bottomless pit, and the smoke of its torment ascend for ever and ever! And having thus, by taking thought, brought my mind into this temper, I once more finally determined to have the clothes, and religiously to observe the compact.

It made me quite happy to end it in this way. The hard bed, the cold night wind blowing on me, my wolfish visitor, were all forgotten. Once more I gave loose to my imagination, and saw myself (clothed and in my right mind) sitting at Yoletta's feet, learning the mystery of that sweet, tranquil life from her precious lips. A whole year was mine in which to love her and win her gentle heart. But her hand—ah, that was another matter. What had I to give in return for such a boon as that? Only that strength concerning which my venerable host had spoken somewhat encouragingly. He had also been so good as to mention my skill; but I could scarcely trade on that. And if a whole year's labour was only sufficient to pay for a suit of clothing, how many years of toil would be required to win Yoletta's hand?

Naturally, at this juncture, I began to draw a parallel between my case and that of an ancient historical personage, whose name is familiar to most. History repeats itself—with variations. Jacob—namely, Smith—cometh to the well of Haran. He taketh acquaintance of Rachel, here called Yoletta. And Jacob kissed Rachel, and lifted up his voice and wept. That is a touch of nature I can thoroughly appreciate—the kissing, I mean; but why he wept I cannot tell, unless it be because he was not an Englishman. And Jacob told Rachel that he was her father's brother. I am glad to have no such startling piece of information to give to the object of *my* affections: we are not even distant relations, and her age being, say, fifteen, and mine twenty-one, we are so far well suited to each other, according to my notions. Smith covenanteth for Yoletta, and said: "I will serve thee seven years for Yoletta, thy younger daughter"; and the old gentleman answered: "Abide with me, for I would rather you should have her than some other person." Now I wonder whether the matter will be complicated with Leah—that is, Edra? Leah was considerably older than Rachel, and, like Edra, tender-eyed. I do not aspire or desire to marry both, especially if I should, like Jacob, have to begin with the wrong one, however tender-eyed: but for divine Yoletta I could serve seven years; yea, and fourteen, if it comes to it.

Thus I mused, and thus I questioned, tossing and turning on my inhospitable hard bed, until merciful sleep laid her quieting hands on the strings of my brain, and hushed their weary jangling.

VIII

FORTUNATELY I woke early next morning, for I was now a member of an early-rising family, and anxious to conform to rules. On going to the door I found, to my inexpressible disgust, that I might easily have closed it in the way I had seen the other door closed, by simply pulling out a sliding panel. There was ventilation enough without having the place open to prowling beasts of prey. I also found that if I had turned up the little straw bed I should have had warm woollen sheets to sleep in.

I resolved to say nothing about my nocturnal visitor, not wishing to begin the day by furnishing fresh instances of what might seem like crass stupidity on my part. While occupied with these matters I began to hear people moving about and talking on the terrace, and peeping out, I beheld a curious and interesting spectacle. Down the broad steps leading to the water the people of the house were hurrying, and flinging themselves like agile, startled frogs on to the bosom of the stream. There, in the midst of his family, my venerable host was already disporting himself, his long, silvery beard and hair floating like a foam on the waves of his own creating. And presently from other sleeping-rooms on a line with mine shot forth new bewitching forms, each sparsely clothed in a slender clinging garment, which concealed no beauteous curve beneath; and nimbly running and leaping down the slope, they quickly joined the masculine bathers.

Looking about I soon found a pretty thing in which to array myself, and quickly started after the others, risking my neck in my desire to imitate the new mode of motion I had just witnessed. The water was delightfully cool and refreshing, and the company very agreeable, ladies and gentlemen all swimming and diving about together with the unconventional freedom and grace of a company of grebes.

After dressing, we assembled in the eating-room or portico where we had supped, just when the red disc of the sun was showing itself above the horizon, kindling the clouds with yellow flame, and filling the green world with new light. I felt happy and strong that morning, very able and willing to work in the fields, and, better than all, very hopeful about that affair of the heart. Happiness, however, is seldom perfect, and in the clear, tender morning light I could not help contrasting my own repulsively ugly garments with the bright and beautiful costumes worn by the others, which seemed to harmonise so well with their fresh, happy morning mood. I also missed the fragrant cup of coffee, the streaky rasher from the dear familiar pig, and, after breakfast, the well-flavoured cigar; but these lesser drawbacks were soon forgotten.

After the meal a small closed basket was handed to me, and one of the young men led me out to a little distance from the house, then, pointing to a belt of wood about a mile away, told me to walk towards it until I came to a ploughed field on the slope of a valley, where I could do some ploughing. Before leaving me he took from his own person a metal dog-whistle, with a string attached, and hung it round my neck, but without explaining its use.

Basket in hand I went away, over the dewy grass, whistling light-heartedly, and after half an hour's walk found the spot indicated, where about an acre and a half of land had been recently turned; there also, lying in the furrow, I found the plough, an implement I knew very little about. This particular plough, however, appeared to be a simple, primitive thing, consisting of a long beam of wood, with an upright pole to guide it; a metal share in the centre, going off to one side, balanced on the other by a couple of small wheels; and there were also some long ropes attached to a cross-stick at the end of the beam. There being no horses or bullocks to do the work, and being unable to draw the plough myself as well as guide it, I sat down leisurely to examine the contents of my basket, which, I found, consisted of brown bread, dried fruit, and a stone bottle of milk. Then, not knowing what else to do, I began to amuse myself by blowing on the whistle, and emitted a most shrill and piercing sound, which very soon produced an unexpected effect. Two noble-looking horses, resembling those I had seen the day before, came galloping towards me as if in response to the sound I had made. Approaching swiftly to within fifty yards they stood still, staring and snorting as if alarmed or astonished, after which they swept round me three or four times, neighing in a sharp, ringing manner, and finally, after having exhausted their superfluous energy, they walked to the plough and placed themselves deliberately before it. It looked as if these animals had come at my call to do the work; I therefore approached them, with more than needful caution, using many soothing, conciliatory sounds and words the while, and after a little further study I discovered how to adjust the ropes to them. There were no blinkers or reins, nor did these superb animals seem to think any were wanted; but after I had taken the pole in my hand, and said "Gee up, Dobbin," in a tone of command, followed by some inarticulate clicks with the tongue, they rewarded me with a disconcerting stare, and then began dragging the plough. As long as I held the pole straight the share cut its way evenly through the mould, but occasionally, owing to my inadvertence, it would go off at a tangent or curve quite out of the ground; and whenever this happened the horses would stop, turn round and stare at me, then, touching their noses together seem to exchange ideas on the subject. When the first furrow was finished, they did not double back, as I expected, but went straight away to a distance of thirty yards, and then, turning, marched back, cutting a fresh furrow parallel with the first, and as straight as a line. Then they returned to the original starting-point and cut another, then again to the new furrow, and so on progressively. All this seemed very wonderful to me, giving the impression that I had been a skilful ploughman all my life without knowing it. It was interesting work; and I was also amused to see the little birds that came in numbers from the wood to devour the worms in the fresh-turned mould; for between their fear of me and their desire to get the worms, they were in a highly perplexed state, and generally confined their operations to one end of the furrow while I was away at the other. The space the horses had marked out for themselves was ploughed up in due time, whereupon they marched off and made a fresh furrow as before, where there was nothing to guide them; and so the work went on agreeably for some hours, until I felt myself growing desperately hungry. Sitting down on the beam of the plough, I opened my basket and discussed the homely fare with a keen appetite.

After finishing the food I resumed work again, but not as cheerfully as at first: I began to feel a little stiff and tired, and the immense quantity of mould adhering to my boots made it heavy walking; moreover, the novelty had now worn off. The horses also did not work as smoothly as at the commencement: they seemed to have something on their minds, for at the end of every furrow they would turn and stare at me in the most exasperating manner.

"Phew!" I ejaculated, as I stood wiping the honest sweat from my face with my mouldy, ancient, and extremely dirty pocket-handkerchief. "Three hundred and sixty-four days of this sort of thing is a rather long price to pay for a suit of clothes."

While standing there, I saw an animal coming swiftly towards me from the direction of the forest, bounding along over the earth with a speed like that of a greyhound—a huge, fierce-looking brute; and when close to me, I felt convinced that it was an animal of the same kind as the one I had seen during the night. Before I had made up my mind what to do, he was within a few yards of me, and then, coming to a sudden halt, he sat down on his haunches, and gravely watched me. Calling to mind some things I had heard about the terrifying effect of the human eye on royal tigers and other savage beasts, I gazed steadily at him, and then almost lost my fear in admiration of his beauty. He was taller than a boarhound, but slender in figure, with keen, fox-like features, and very large, erect ears; his coat was silvery-grey, and long; there were two black spots above his eyes; and the feet, muzzle, ear-tips, and end of the bushy tail were also velvet-black. After watching me quietly for two or three minutes, he started up, and, much to my relief, trotted away towards the wood; but after going about fifty yards he looked back, and seeing me still gazing after him, wheeled round and rushed at me, and when quite close uttered a sound like a ringing, metallic yelp, after which he once more bounded away, and disappeared from sight.

The horses now turned round, and, deliberately walking up to me, stood still, in spite of all I could do to make them continue the work. After waiting a while they proceeded to wriggle themselves out of the ropes, and galloped off, loudly neighing to each other, and flinging up their disdainful heels so as to send a shower of dirt over me. Left alone in this unceremonious fashion, I presently began to think that they knew more about the work than I did, and that, finding me indisposed to release them at the proper moment, they had taken the matter into their own hands, or hoofs rather. A little more pondering, and I also came to the conclusion that the singular wolf-like animal was only one of the house-dogs; that he had visited me in the night to remind me that I was sleeping with the door open, and had come now to insist on a suspension of work.

Glad at having discovered all these things without displaying my ignorance by asking questions, I took up my basket and started home.

IX

WHEN I arrived at the house I was met by the young man who had set me the morning's task; but he was taciturn now, and wore a cold, estranged look, which seemed to portend trouble. He at once led me to a part of the house at a distance from the hall, and into a large apartment I now saw for the first time. In a few moments the master of the house, followed by most of the other inmates, also entered, and on the faces of all of them I noticed the same cold, offended look.

"The dickens take my luck!" said I to myself, beginning to feel extremely uncomfortable. "I suppose I have offended against the laws and customs by working the horses too long."

"Smith," said the old man, advancing to the table, and depositing thereon a large volume he had brought with him, "come here, and read to me in this book."

Advancing to the table, I saw that it was written in the same minute, Hebrew-like characters of the folio I had examined on the previous evening. "I cannot read it; I do not understand the letters," I said, feeling some shame at having thus publicly to confess my ignorance.

"Then," said he, bending on me a look of the utmost severity, "there is indeed little more to be said. Nevertheless, we take into account the confused state of your intellect yesterday, and judge you leniently; and let us hope that the pangs of an outraged conscience will be more painful to you than the light punishment I am about to inflict for so detestable a crime."

I now concluded that I had offended by squeezing Yoletta's hand, and had been told to read from the book merely to make myself acquainted with the pains and penalties attendant on such an indiscretion, for to call it a "detestable crime" seemed to me a very great abuse of language.

"If I have offended," was my answer, delivered with little humility, "I can only plead my ignorance of the customs of the house."

"No man," he returned, with increased severity, "is so ignorant as not to know right from wrong. Had the matter come to my knowledge sooner, I should have said: Depart from us, for your continued presence in the house offends us; but we have made a compact with you, and, until the year expires, we must suffer you. For the space of sixty days you must dwell apart from us, never leaving the room, where each day a task will be assigned to you, and subsisting on bread and water only. Let us hope that in this period of solitude and silence you will sufficiently repent your crime, and rejoin us afterwards with a changed heart; for all offences may be forgiven a man, but it is impossible to forgive a lie."

"A lie!" I exclaimed in amazement. "I have told no lie!"

"This," said he, with an access of wrath, "is an aggravation of your former offence. It is even a worse offence than the first, and must be dealt with separately—when the sixty days have expired."

"Are you, then, going to condemn me without hearing me speak, or telling me anything about it? What lie have I told?"

After a pause, during which he closely scrutinised my face, he said, pointing to the open page before him, "Yesterday, in answer to my question, you told me that you could read. Last evening you made a contrary statement to Yoletta; and now here is the book, and you confess that you cannot read it."

"But that is easily explained," said I, immensely relieved, for I certainly had felt a little guilty about the hand-squeezing performance, although it was not a very serious matter. "I can read the books of my own country, and naturally concluded that your books were written in the same kind of letters; but last evening I discovered that it was not so. You have already seen the letters of my country on the coins I showed you last evening."

And here I again pulled out my pocket-book, and emptied the contents on the table.

He began to pick up the sovereigns one by one to examine them. Meanwhile, finding my beautiful black and gold stylograph pen inserted in the book, I thought I could not do better than to show him how I wrote. Fortunately, the fluid in it had not become dry. Tearing a blank page from my book I hastily scribbled a few lines, and handed the paper to him, saying: "This is how I write."

He began studying the paper, but his eyes, I perceived, wandered often to the stylograph pen in my hand.

Presently he remarked: "This writing, or these marks you have made on the paper, are not the same as the letters on the gold."

I took the paper and proceeded to copy the sentence I had written, but in printing letters, beneath it, then returned it to him.

He examined it again, and, after comparing my letters with those on the sovereigns, said: "Pray tell me, now, what you have written here, and explain why you write in two different ways?"

I told him, as well as I could, why letters of one form were used to stamp on gold and other substances, and of a different form for writing. Then, with a modest blush, I read the words of the sentence: "In different parts of the world men have different customs, and write different letters; but alike to all men, in all places, a lie is hateful."

"Smith," he said, addressing me in an impressive manner, but happily not to charge me with a *third* and bigger lie, "I have lived long in the world, and the knowledge others possess concerning it is mine also. It is common knowledge that in the hotter and colder regions men are compelled to live differently, owing to the conditions they are placed in; but we know that everywhere they have the same law of right and wrong inscribed on the heart, and, as you have said, hate a lie; also that they all speak the same language; and until this moment I also believed that they wrote in similar characters. You, however, have now succeeded in convincing me that this is not the case; that in some obscure valley, cut off from all intercourse by inaccessible mountains, or in some small, unknown island of the sea, a people may exist—ah, did you not tell me that you came from an island?"

"Yes, my home was on an island," I answered.

"So I imagined. An island of which no report has ever reached us, where the people, isolated from their fellows, have in the course of many centuries changed their customs—even their manner of writing. Although I had seen these gold pieces I did not understand, or did not realise, that such a human family existed: now I am persuaded of it, and as I alone am to blame for having brought this charge against you, I must now ask your forgiveness. We rejoice at your innocence, and hope with increased love to atone for our injustice. My son," he concluded, placing a hand on my shoulder, "I am now deeply in your debt."

"I am glad it has ended so happily," I replied, wondering whether his being in my debt would increase my chances with Yoletta or not.

Seeing him again directing curious glances at the stylograph, which I was turning about in my fingers, I offered it to him.

He examined it with interest.

"I have only been waiting for an opportunity," he said, "to look closely at this wonderful contrivance, for I had perceived that your writing was not made with a pencil, but with a fluid. It is black polished stone, beautifully fashioned and encircled with gold bands, and contains the writing-fluid within itself. This surprises me as much as anything you have told me."

"Allow me to make you a present of it," said I, seeing him so taken with it.

"No, not so," he returned. "But I should greatly like to possess it, and will keep it if I may bestow in return something you desire."

Yoletta's hand was really the only thing in life I desired, but it was too early to speak yet, as I knew nothing about their matrimonial usages—not even whether or not the lady's consent was necessary to a compact of the kind. I therefore made a more modest request. "There is one thing I greatly desire," I said. "I am very anxious to be able to read in your books, and shall consider myself more than compensated if you will permit Yoletta to teach me."

"She shall teach you in any case, my son," he returned. "That, and much more, is already owing to you."

"There is nothing else I desire," said I. "Pray keep the pen and make me happy."

And thus ended a disagreeable matter.

The cloud having blown over, we all repaired to the supper-room, and nothing could exceed our happiness as we sat at meat—or vegetables. Not feeling so ravenously hungry as on the previous evening, and, moreover, seeing them all in so lively a mood, I did not hesitate to join in the conversation: nor did I succeed so very badly, considering the strangeness of it all; for like the bee that has been much hindered at his flowery work by geometric webs, I began to acquire some skill in pushing my way gracefully through the tangling meshes of thought and phrases that were new to me.

The afternoon's experiences had certainly been remarkable—a strange mixture of pain and pleasure, not blending into homogeneous grey, but resembling rather a bright embroidery on a dark, sombre ground; and of these surprising contrasts I was destined to have more that same evening.

We were again assembled in the great room, the venerable father reclining at his ease on his throne-like couch near the brass globes, while the others pursued their various occupations as on the former evening. Not being able to get near Yoletta, and having nothing to do, I settled myself comfortably in one of the spacious seats, and gave up my mind to pleasant dreams. At length, to my surprise, the father, who had been regarding me for some time, said: "Will you lead, my son?"

I started up, turning very red in the face, for I did not wish to trouble him with questions, yet was at a loss to know what he meant by leading. I thought of several things—whist, evening prayers, dancing, etc.; but being still in doubt, I was compelled to ask him to explain.

"Will you lead the singing?" he returned, looking a little surprised.

"Oh yes, with pleasure," said I. There being no music about, and no piano, I concluded naturally that my friends amused themselves with solo songs without accompaniment of an evening, and having a good tenor voice I was not unwilling to lead off with a song. Clearing my rusty throat with a *ghrr-ghrr-hram* which made them all jump, I launched forth with "The Vicar of Bray"—a grand old song and a great favourite of mine. They all started when I commenced, exchanging glances, and casting astonished looks towards me; but it was getting so dusky in the room that I could not feel sure that my eyes were not deceiving me. Presently some that were near me began retiring to distant seats, and this distressed me so that it made me hoarse, and my singing became very bad indeed; but still I thought it best to go bravely on to the end. Suddenly the old gentleman, who had been staring wildly at me for some time, drew up his long yellow robe and wrapped it round his face and head. I glanced at Yoletta, sitting at some distance, and saw that she was holding her hands pressed to her ears.

I thought it about time to leave off then, and stopping abruptly in the middle of the fourth stanza I sat down, feeling extremely hot and uncomfortable. I was almost choking, and unable to utter a word. But there was no word for me to utter: it was, of course, for them to thank me for singing, or to say something; but not a word was spoken. Yoletta dropped her hands and resumed her work, while the old man slowly emerged with a somewhat frightened look from the wrappings; and then the long dead silence becoming unendurable, I remarked that I feared my singing was not to their taste. No reply was made; only the father, putting out one of his hands, touched a handle or key near him, whereupon one of the brass globes began slowly revolving. A low murmur of sound arose, and seemed to pass like a wave through the room, dying away in the distance, soon to be succeeded by another, and then another, each marked by an increase of power; and often as this solemn sound died away, faint flute-like notes were heard as if approaching, but still at a great distance, and in the ensuing wave of sound from the great globes they would cease to be distinguishable. Still the mysterious coming sounds continued at intervals to grow louder and clearer, joined by other tones as they progressed, now altogether bursting out in joyous chorus, then one purest liquid note soaring bird-like alone, but whether from voices or wind-instruments I was unable to tell, until the whole air about me was filled and palpitating with the strange, exquisite harmony, which passed onwards, the tones growing fewer and fainter by degrees until they almost died out of hearing in the opposite direction. That all were now taking part in the performance I became convinced by watching in turn different individuals, some of them having small, curiously-shaped instruments in their hands, but there was a blending of voices and a something like ventriloquism in the tones which made it impossible to distinguish the notes of any one person. Deeper, more sonorous tones now issued from the revolving globes, sometimes resembling in character the *vox humana* of an organ, and every time they rose to a certain pitch there were responsive sounds—not certainly from any of the performers—low, tremulous, and Æolian in character, wandering over the entire room, as if walls and ceiling were honeycombed with sensitive musical cells, answering to the deeper vibrations. These floating aerial sounds also answered to the higher notes of some of the female singers, resembling soprano voices, brightened and spiritualised in a wonderful degree; and then the wide room would be filled with a mist, as it were, of this floating, formless melody, which seemed to come from invisible harpers hovering in the shadows above.

Lying back on my couch, listening with closed eyes to this mysterious, soul-stirring concert, I was affected to tears, and almost feared that I had been snatched away into some supra-mundane region inhabited by beings of an angelic or half-angelic order—*feared*, I say, for, with this new love in my heart, no elysium or starry abode could compare with this green earth for a dwelling-place. But when I remembered my own brutal bull of Bashan performance, my face, there in the dark, was on fire with shame; and I cursed the ignorant, presumptuous folly I had been guilty of in roaring out that abominable "Vicar of Bray" ballad, which had now become as hateful to me as my trousers or boots. The composer of that song, the writer of the words, and its subject, the double-faced Vicar himself, presented themselves to my mind as the three most damnable beings that had ever existed. "The devil take my luck!" I muttered, grinding my teeth with impotent anger; for it seemed such hard lines, just when I had succeeded in getting into favour, to go and spoil it all in that unhappy way. Now that I had become acquainted with *their* style of singing, the supposed fib, about which there had been such a pother, seemed a very venial offence compared with my attempt to *lead the singing*. Nevertheless, when the concert was over, not a word was said on the subject by any one, though I had quite expected to be taken at once to the magisterial chamber to hear some dreadful sentence passed on me; and when, before retiring, anxious to propitiate my host, I began to express regret for having inflicted pain on them by attempting to sing, the venerable gentleman raised his hands deprecatingly, and begged me to say no more about it, for painful subjects were best forgotten. "No doubt," he kindly added, "when you were lying there buried among the hills, you swallowed a large amount of earth and gravel in your efforts to breathe, and have not yet freed your lungs from it."

This was the most charitable view he could take of the matter, and I was thankful that no worse result followed.

X

AT length the joyful day arrived when I was to cease, in outward appearance at all events, to be an alien; for returning at noon from the fields, on entering my cell I beheld my beautiful new garments—two complete suits, besides underwear: one, the most soberly coloured, intended only for working hours; but the second, which was for the house, claimed my first attention. Trembling with eagerness, I flung off the old tweeds, the cracked boots, and other vestiges of a civilisation which they had perhaps survived, and soon found that I had been measured with faultless accuracy; for everything, down to the shoes, fitted to perfection. Green was the prevailing or ground tint—a soft sap green; the pattern on it, which was very beautiful, being a somewhat obscure red, inclining to purple. My delight culminated when I drew on the hose, which had, like those worn by the others, a curious design, evidently borrowed from the skin of some kind of snake. The ground colour was light green, almost citron yellow, in fact, and the pattern a bright maroon red, with bronze reflections.

I had no sooner arrayed myself than, with a flushed face and palpitating heart, I flew to exhibit myself to my friends, and found them assembled and waiting to see and admire the result of their work. The pleasure I saw reflected in their transparent faces increased my happiness a hundredfold, and I quite astonished them with the torrent of eloquence in which I expressed my overflowing gratitude.

"Now, tell me one secret," I exclaimed, when the excitement began to abate a little. "Why is green the principal colour in my clothes, when no other person in the house wears more than a very little of it?"

I had no sooner spoken than I heartily wished that I had held my peace; for it all at once occurred to me that green was perhaps the colour for an alien or mere hireling, in which light they perhaps regarded me.

"Oh, Smith, can you not guess so simple a thing?" said Edra, placing her white hands on my shoulders and smiling straight into my face.

How beautiful she looked, standing there with her eyes so near to mine! "Tell me why, Edra?" I said, still with a lingering apprehension.

"Why, look at the colour of my eyes and skin—would this green tint be suitable for me to wear?"

"Oh, is that the reason!" cried I, immensely relieved. "I think, Edra, you would look very beautiful in any colour that is on the earth, or in the rainbow above the earth. But am I so different from you all?"

"Oh yes, quite different—have you never looked at yourself? Your skin is whiter and redder, and your hair has a very different colour. It will look better when it grows long, I think. And your eyes—do you know that they never change! for when we look at you closely they are still blue-grey, and not green."

"No; I wish they were," said I. "Now I shall value my clothes a hundred times more, since you have taken so much pains to make them—well, what shall I say?—harmonise, I suppose, with the peculiar colour of my mug. Dash it all, I'm blundering again! I mean—I mean—don't you know——"

Edra laughed and gave it up. Then we all laughed; for now evidently my blundering did not so much matter, since I had shed my outer integument, and come forth like a snake (with a divided tail) in a brand new skin.

Presently I missed Yoletta from the room, and desiring above all things to have some word of congratulation from her lips, I went off to seek her. She was standing under the portico waiting for me. "Come," she said, and proceeded to lead me into the music-room, where we sat down on one of the couches close to the daïs; there she produced some large white tablets, and red chalk pencils or crayons.

"Now, Smith, I am going to begin teaching you," said she, with the grave air of a young schoolmistress; "and every afternoon, when your work is done, you must come to me here."

"I hope I am very stupid, and that it will take me a long time to learn," said I.

"Oh"—she laughed—"do you think it will be so pleasant sitting by me here? I am glad you think that; but if you prefer me for a teacher you must not try to be stupid, because if you do I shall ask some one else to take my place."

"Would you really do that, Yoletta?"

"Yes. Shall I tell you why? Because I have a quick, impatient temper. Everything wrong I have ever done, for which I have been punished, has been through my hasty temper."

"And have you ever undergone that sad punishment of being shut up by yourself for many days, Yoletta?"

"Yes, often; for what other punishment is there? But oh, I hope it will never happen again, because I think—I know that I suffer more than any one can imagine. To tread on the grass, to feel the sun and wind on my face, to see the earth and sky and animals—this is like life to me; and when I am shut up alone, every day seems—oh, a year at least!" She did not know how much dearer this confession of one little human weakness made her seem to me. "Come, let us begin," she said. "I waited for your new clothes to be finished, and we must make up for lost time."

"But do you know, Yoletta, that you have not said anything about them? Do I look nice; and will you like me any better now?"

"Yes, much better. You were a poor caterpillar before; I liked you a little because I knew what a pretty butterfly you would be in time. I helped to make your wings. Now, listen."

For two hours she taught me, making her red letters or marks, which I copied on my tablet, and explaining them to me; and at the conclusion of the lesson, I had got a general idea that the writing was to a great extent phonographic, and that I was in for rather a tough job.

"Do you think that you will be able to teach me to sing also?" I asked, when she had put the tablets aside.

The memory of that miserable failure, when I "had led the singing," was a constant sore in my mind. I had begun to think that I had not done myself justice on that memorable occasion, and the desire to make another trial under more favourable circumstances was very strong in me.

She looked a little startled at my question, but said nothing.

"I know now," I continued pleadingly, "that you all sing softly. If you will only consent to try me once I promise to stick like cobbler's wax—I beg your pardon, I mean I will endeavour to adhere to the *morendo* and *perdendosi* style—don't you know? What *am* I saying! But I promise you, Yoletta, I shan't frighten you, if you will only let me try and sing to you once."

She turned from me with a somewhat clouded expression of face, and walked with slow steps to the daïs, and placing her hands on the keys, caused two of the small globes to revolve, sending soft waves of sound through the room.

I advanced towards her, but she raised her hand apprehensively. "No, no, no; stand there," she said, "and sing low."

It was hard to see her troubled face and obey, but I was not going to bellow at her like a bull, and I had set my heart on this trial. For the last three days, while working in the fields, I had been incessantly practising my dear old master Campana's exquisite *M'appar sulla tomba,* the only melody I happened to know which had any resemblance to their divine music. To my surprise she seemed to play as I sang a suitable accompaniment on the globes, which aided and encouraged me, and, although singing in a subdued tone, I felt that I had never sung so well before. When I finished, I quite expected some word of praise, or to be asked why I had not sung this melody on that unhappy evening when I was asked to lead; but she spoke no word.

"Will you sing something now?" I said.

"Not now—this evening," she replied absently, slowly walking across the floor with eyes cast down.

"What are you thinking of, Yoletta, that you look so serious?" I asked.

"Nothing," she returned, a little impatiently.

"You look very solemn about nothing, then. But you have not said one word about my singing—did you not like it?"

"Your singing? Oh no! It was a pleasant-tasting little kernel in a very rough rind—I should like one without the other."

"You talk in riddles, Yoletta; but I'm afraid the answers to them would not sound very flattering to me. But if you would like to know the song I shall be only too glad to teach it to you. The words are in Italian, but I can translate them."

"The words?" she said absently.

"The words of the song," I said.

"I do not know what you mean by the words of a song. Do not speak to me now, Smith."

"Oh, very well," said I, thinking it all very strange, and sitting down I divided my attention between my beautiful hose and Yoletta, still slowly pacing the floor with that absent look on her face.

At length the curious mood changed, but I did not venture to talk any more about music, and before very long we repaired to the eating-room, where, for the next two or three hours, we occupied ourselves very agreeably with those processes which, some new theorist informs us, constitute our chief pleasure in life.

That evening I overheard a curious little dialogue. The father of the house, as I had now grown accustomed to call our head, after rising from his seat, stood for a few minutes talking near me, while Yoletta, with her hand on his arm, waited for him to finish. When he had done speaking, and turned to her, she said in a low voice, which I, however, overheard, "Father, I shall lead to-night."

He put his hand on her head, and, looking down, studied her upturned face. "Ah, my daughter," he said with a smile, "shall I guess what has inspired you to-day? You have been listening to the passage birds. I also heard them this morning passing in flocks. And you have been following them in thought far away into those sun-bright lands where winter never comes."

"No, father," she returned, "I have only been a little way from home in thought—only to that spot where the grass has not yet grown to hide the ashes and loose mould."

He stooped and kissed her forehead, and then left the room; and she, never noticing the hungry look with which I witnessed the tender caress, also went away.

That some person was supposed to lead the singing every evening I knew, but it was impossible for me ever to discover who the leader was; now, however, after over-hearing this conversation, I knew that on this particular occasion it would be Yoletta, and in spite of the very poor opinion she had expressed of my musical abilities, I was prepared to admire the performance more than I had ever done before.

It commenced in the usual mysterious and indefinable manner; but after a time, when it began to shape itself into melodies, the idea possessed me that I was listening to strains once familiar, but long unheard and forgotten. At length I discovered that this was Campana's music, only not as I had ever heard it sung; for the melody of *M'appar sulla tomba* had been so transmuted and etherealised, as it were, that the composer himself would have listened in wondering ecstasy to the mournful strains, which had passed through the alembic of their more delicately organised minds. Listening, I remembered with an unaccountable feeling of sadness, that poor Campana had recently died in London; and almost at the same moment there came to me a remembrance of my beloved mother, whose early death was my first great grief in boyhood. All the songs I had ever heard her sing came back to me, ringing in my mind with a wonderful joy, but ever ending in a strange, funereal sadness. And not only my mother, but many a dear one besides returned "in beauty from the dust" appeared to be present—white-haired old men who had spoken treasured words to me in bygone years; schoolfellows and other boyish friends and companions; and men, too, in the prime of life, of whose premature death in this or that far-off region of the world-wide English empire I had heard from time to time. They came back to me, until the whole room seemed filled with a pale, shadowy procession, moving past me to the sound of that mysterious melody. Through all the evening it came back, in a hundred bewildering disguises, filling me with a melancholy infinitely precious, which was yet almost more than my heart could bear. Again and yet again that despairing *Ah-i-me* fell like a long shuddering sob from the revolving globes, and from voices far and near, to be taken up and borne yet further away by far-off, dying sounds, yet again responded to by nearer, clearer voices, in tones which seemed wrung "from the depths of some divine despair"; then to pass away, but not wholly pass, for all the hidden cells were stirred, and the vibrating air, like mysterious, invisible hands, swept the suspended strings, until the exquisite bliss and pain of it made me tremble and shed tears, as I sat there in the dark, wondering, as men will wonder at such moments, what this tempest of the soul which music wakes in us can mean: whether it is merely a growth of this our earth-life, or a something added, a divine hunger of the heart which is part of our immortality.

XI

IT seemed to me now that I had never really lived before, so sweet was this new life—so healthy, and free from care and regret. The old life, which I had lived in cities, was less in my thoughts on each succeeding day; it came to me now like the memory of a repulsive dream, which I was only too glad to forget. How I had ever found that listless, worn-out, luxurious, do-nothing existence endurable, seemed a greater mystery every morning, when I went forth to my appointed task in the fields or the workhouse, so natural and so pleasant did it now seem to labour with my own hands, and to eat my bread in the sweat of my face. If there was one kind of work I preferred above all others, it was wood-cutting, and as a great deal of timber was required at this season, I was allowed to follow my own inclination. In the forest, a couple of miles from the house, several tough old giants—chiefly oak, chestnut, elm, and beech—had been marked out for destruction: in some cases because they had been scorched and riven by lightnings, and were an eyesore; in others, because time had robbed them of their glory, withering their long, desolate arms, and bestowing on their crowns that lustreless, scanty foliage which has a mournful meaning, like the thin white hairs on the bowed head of a very old man. At this distance from the house I could freely indulge my propensity for singing, albeit in that coarser tone which had failed to win favour with my new friends. Among the grand trees, out of earshot of them all, I could shout aloud to my heart's content, rejoicing in the boisterous old English ballads, which, like John Peele's view-hallo,

"Might awaken the dead
Or the fox from his lair in the morning."

Meanwhile, with the frantic energy of a Gladstone out of office, I plied my axe, its echoing strokes making fit accompaniment to my strains, until for many yards about me the ground was littered with white and yellow chips; then, exhausted with my efforts, I would sit down to rest and eat my simple mid-day fare, to admire myself in my deep green and chocolate working-dress, and, above everything, to think and dream of Yoletta.

In my walks to and from the forest I cast many a wistful look at a solitary flat-topped hill, almost a mountain in height, which stood two or three miles from the house, north of it, on the other side of the river. From its summit I felt sure that a very extensive view of the surrounding country might be had, and I often wished to pay this hill a visit. One afternoon, while taking my lesson in reading, I mentioned this desire to Yoletta.

"Come, then, let us go there now," said she, laying the tablets aside.

I joyfully agreed: I had never walked alone with her, nor, in fact, with her at all, since that first day when she had placed her hand in mine; and now we were so much nearer in heart to each other.

She led me to a point, half a mile from the house, where the stream rushed noisily over its stony bed and formed numerous deep channels between the rocks, and one could cross over by jumping from rock to rock. Yoletta led the way, leaping airily from stone to stone, while I, anxious to escape a wetting, followed her with caution; but when I was safe over, and thought our delightful walk was about to begin, she suddenly started off towards the hill at a swift pace, which quickly left me far behind. Finding that I could not overtake her, I shouted to her to wait for me; then she stood still until I was within three or four yards of her, when off she fled like the wind once more. At length she reached the foot of the hill, and sat down there until I joined her.

"For goodness sake, Yoletta, let us behave like rational beings and walk quietly," I was beginning, when away she went again, dancing up the mountain-side with a tireless energy that amazed as well as exasperated me. "Wait for me just once more," I screamed after her; then, half-way up the side, she stopped and sat down on a stone.

"Now my chance has come," thought I, ready to make up for insufficient speed and wind by superior cunning, which would make us equal. "I will go quietly up and catch her napping, and hold her fast by the arm until the walk is finished. So far it has been nothing but a mad chase."

Slowly I toiled on, and then, when I got near her and was just about to execute my plan, she started nimbly away, with a merry laugh, and never paused again until the summit was reached. Thoroughly tired and beaten, I sat down to rest; but presently looking up I saw her at the top, standing motionless on a stone, looking like a statue outlined against the clear blue sky. Once more I got up and pressed on until I reached her, and then sank down on the grass, overcome with fatigue.

"When you ask me to walk again, Yoletta," I panted, "I shall not move unless I have a rope round your waist to pull you back when you try to rush off in that mad fashion. You have knocked all the wind out of me; and yet I was in pretty good trim."

She laughed, and jumping to the ground, sat down at my side on the grass.

I caught her hand and held it tight. "Now you shall not escape and run away again," said I.

"You may keep my hand," she replied; "it has nothing to do up here."

"May I put it to some useful purpose—may I do what I like with it?"

"Yes, you may," then she added with a smile: "There is no thorn in it now."

I kissed it many times on the back, the palm, the wrist, then bestowed a separate caress on each finger-tip.

"Why do you kiss my hand?" she asked.

"Do you not know—can you not guess? Because it is the sweetest thing I can kiss, except one other thing. Shall I tell you——"

"My face? And why do you not kiss that?"

"Oh, may I?" said I, and drawing her to me I kissed her soft cheek. "May I kiss the other cheek now?" I asked. She turned it to me, and when I had kissed it rapturously, I gazed into her eyes, which looked back, bright and unabashed, into mine. "I think—I think I made a slight mistake, Yoletta," I said. "What I meant to ask was, will you let me kiss you where I like—on your chin, for instance, or just where I like?"

"Yes; but you are keeping me too long. Kiss me as many times as you like, and then let us admire the prospect."

I drew her closer and kissed her mouth, not once nor twice, but clinging to it with all the ardour of passion, as if my lips had become glued to hers.

Suddenly she disengaged herself from me. "Why do you kiss my mouth in that violent way?" she exclaimed, her eyes sparkling, her cheeks flushed. "You seem like some hungry animal that wanted to devour me."

That was, oddly enough, just how I felt. "Do you not know, sweetest, why I kiss you in that way? Because I love you."

"I know you do, Smith. I can understand and appreciate your love without having my lips bruised."

"And do you love me, Yoletta?"

"Yes, certainly—did you not know that?"

"And is it not sweet to kiss when you love? Do you know what love is, darling? Do you love me a thousand times more than any one else in the world?"

"How extravagantly you talk!" she replied. "What strange things you say!"

"Yes, dear, because love is strange—the strangest, sweetest thing in life. It comes once only to the heart, and the one person loved is infinitely more than all others. Do you not understand that?"

"Oh no; what do you mean, Smith?"

"Is there any other person dearer to your heart than I am?"

"I love every one in the house, some more than others. Those that are closely related to me I love most."

"Oh, please say no more! You love your people with one kind of love, but me with a different love—is it not so?"

"There is only one kind of love," said she.

"Ah, you say that because you are a child yet, and do not know. You are even younger than I thought, perhaps. How old are you, dear?"

"Thirty-one years old," she replied, with the utmost gravity.

"Oh, Yoletta, what an awful cram! I mean—oh, I beg your pardon for being so rude! But—but don't you think you can draw it mild? Thirty-one—what a joke! Why, I'm an old fellow compared with you, and I'm not twenty-two yet. Do tell me what you mean, Yoletta?"

She was not listening to me, I saw: she had risen from the grass and seated herself again on the stone. For only answer to my question she pointed to the west with her hand, saying: "Look there, Smith."

I stood up and looked. The sun was near the horizon now, and partially concealed by low clouds, which were beginning to form—grey, and tinged with purple and red; but their misty edges burned with an intense yellow flame. Above, the sky was clear as blue glass, barred with pale-yellow rays, shot forth by the sinking sun, and resembling the spokes of an immense celestial wheel reaching to the zenith. The billowy earth, with its forests in deep green and many-coloured, autumnal foliage, stretched far before us, here in shadow, and there flushed with rich light; while the mountain range, looming near and stupendous on our sight, had changed its colour from dark blue to violet.

The doubts and fears agitating my heart made me indifferent to the surpassing beauty of the scene: I turned impatiently from it to gaze again on her graceful figure, girlish still in its slim proportions; but her face, flushed with sunlight, and crowned with its dark, shining hair, seemed to me like the face of one of the immortals. The expression of rapt devotion on it made me silent, for it seemed as if she too had been touched by nature's magic, like earth and sky, and been transfigured; and waiting for the mood to pass, I stood by her side, resting my hand on her knee. By-and-by she looked down and smiled, and then I returned to the subject of her age.

"Surely, Yoletta," said I, "you were only poking fun at me—I mean, amusing yourself at my expense. You can't possibly be more than about fifteen, or sixteen at the very outside."

She smiled again and shook her head.

"Oh, I know, I can solve the riddle now. Your years are different, of course, like everything else in this latitude. A month is called a year with you, and that would make you, let me see—how much is twelve times thirty-one? Oh, hang it, nearly five hundred, I should think. Why am I such a duffer at mental arithmetic! It is just the contrary—how many twelves in thirty-one? About two and a half in round numbers, and that's absurd, as you are not a baby. Oh, I have it: your seasons are called years, of course—why didn't I see it before! No, that would make you only seven and a half. Ah, yes, I see it now: a year means two years, or two of your years—summer and winter—mean a year; and that just makes you sixteen, exactly what I had imagined. Is it not so, Yoletta?"

"I do not know what you are talking about, Smith; and I am not listening."

"Well, listen for one moment, and tell me how long does a year last?"

"It lasts from the time the leaves fall in the autumn until they fall again; and it lasts from the time the swallows come in spring until they come again."

"And seriously, honestly, you are thirty-one years old?"

"Did I not tell you so? Yes, I am thirty-one years old."

"Well, I never heard anything to equal this! Good heavens, what does it mean? I know it is awfully rude to enquire a lady's age, but what am I to do? Will you kindly tell me Edra's age?"

"Edra? I forget. Oh yes; she is sixty-three."

"Sixty-three! I'll be shot if she's a day more than twenty-eight! Idiot that I am, why can't I keep calm! But, Yoletta, how you distress me! It almost frightens me to ask another question, but do tell me how old your father is?"

"He is nearly two hundred years old—a hundred and ninety-eight, I think," she replied.

"Heavens on earth—I shall go stark, staring mad!" But I could say no more; leaving her side I sat down on a low stone at some distance, with a stunned feeling in my brain, and something like despair in my heart. That she had told me the truth I could no longer doubt for one moment: it was impossible for her crystal nature to be anything but truthful. The number of her years mattered nothing to me; the virgin sweetness of girlhood was on her lips, the freshness and glory of early youth on her forehead; the misery was that she had lived thirty-one years in the world and did not understand the words I had spoken to her—did not know what love, or passion, was! Would it always be so—would my heart consume itself to ashes, and kindle no fire in hers?

Then, as I sat there, filled with these despairing thoughts, she came down from her perch, and, dropping on her knees before me, put her arms about my neck and gazed steadily into my face. "Why are you troubled, Smith—have I said anything to hurt you?" said she. "And do you not know that you have offended me?"

"Have I? Tell me how, dearest Yoletta."

"By asking questions, and saying wild, meaningless things while I sat there watching the setting sun. It troubled me and spoiled my pleasure; but I will forgive you, Smith, because I love you. Do you not think I love you enough? You are very dear to me—dearer every day." And drawing down my face she kissed my lips.

"Darling, you make me happy again," I returned, "for if your love increases every day, the time will perhaps come when you will understand me, and be all I wish to me."

"What is it that you wish?" she questioned.

"That you should be mine—mine alone, wholly mine—and give yourself to me, body and soul."

She continued gazing up into my eyes. "In a sense we do, I suppose, give ourselves, body and soul, to those we love," she said. "And if you are not yet satisfied that I have given myself to you in that way, you must wait patiently, saying and doing nothing wilfully to alienate my heart, until the time arrives when my love will be equal to your desire. Come," she added, and, rising, pulled me up by the hand.

Silently, and somewhat pensively, we started hand in hand on our walk down the hill. Presently she dropped on her knees, and opening the grass with her hands, displayed a small, slender bud, on a round, smooth stem, springing without leaves from the soil. "Do you see!" she said, looking up at me with a bright smile.

"Yes, dear, I see a bud; but I do not know anything more about it."

"Oh, Smith, do you not know that it is a rainbow lily!" And rising, she took my hand and walked on again.

"What is the rainbow lily?"

"By-and-by, in a few days, it will be in fullest bloom, and the earth will be covered with its glory."

"It is so late in the season, Yoletta! Spring is the time to see the earth covered with the glory of flowers."

"There is nothing to equal the rainbow lily, which comes when most flowers are dead, or have their bright colours tarnished. Have you lived in the moon, Smith, that I have to tell you these things?"

"No, dear, but in that island where all things, including flowers, were different."

"Ah, yes; tell me about the island."

Now "that island" was an unfortunate subject, and I was not prepared to break the resolution I had made of prudently holding my tongue about its peculiar institutions. "How can I tell you?—how could you imagine it if I were to tell you?" I said, evading the question. "You have seen the heavens black with tempests, and have felt the lightnings blinding your eyes, and have heard the crash of the thunder: could you imagine all that if you had never witnessed it, and I described it to you?"

"No."

"Then it would be useless to tell you. And now tell me about the rainbow lilies, for I am a great lover of flowers."

"Are you? Is it strange you should have a taste common to all human beings?" she returned with a pretty smile. "But it is easier to ask questions than to answer them. If you had never seen the sun setting in glory, or the midnight sky shining with myriads of stars, could you imagine these things if I described them to you?"

"No."

"That word is an echo, Smith. You must wait for the earth to bring forth her rainbow lilies, and the heart its love."

"With or without flowers, the world is a paradise to me, with you at my side, Yoletta. Ah, if you will be my Eve! How sweet it is to walk hand in hand with you in the twilight; but it was not so nice when you were scuttling from me like a wild rabbit. I'm glad to find that you do walk sometimes."

"Yes, sometimes—on solemn occasions."

"Yes? Tell me about these solemn occasions."

"This is not one of them," she replied, suddenly withdrawing her hand from mine; then with a ringing laugh, she sped from me, bounding down the hill-side with the speed and grace of a gazelle.

I instantly gave chase; but it was a very vain chase, although I put forth all my powers. Occasionally she would drop on her knees to admire some wild flower, or search for a lily bud; and whenever she came to a large stone, she would spring on to it, and stand for some time motionless, gazing at the rich hues of the afterglow; but always at my approach she would spring lightly away, escaping from me as easily as a wild bird. Tired with running, I at last gave up the hunt, and walked soberly home by myself, wondering whether that conversation on the summit of the hill, and all the curious information I had gathered from it, should make me the most miserable or the most happy being upon earth.

XII

THE question whether I had reason to feel happy or the reverse still occupied me after going to bed, and kept me awake far into the night. I put it to myself in a variety of ways, concentrating my faculties on it; but the result still remained doubtful. Mine was a curious position for a man to be in; for here was I, very much in love with Yoletta, who said that her age was thirty-one, and yet who knew of only one kind of love—that sisterly affection which she gave me so unstintingly. Of course I was surrounded with mysteries, being in the house but not of it, to the manner born; and I had already arrived at the conclusion that these mysteries could only be known to me through reading, once that accomplishment was mine. For it seemed rather a dangerous thing to ask questions, since the most innocent interrogatory might be taken as an offence, only to be expiated by solitary confinement and a bread-and-water diet; or, if not punishable in that way, it would probably be regarded as a result of the supposed collision of my head with a stone. To be reticent, observant, and studious was a safe plan; this had served to make me diligent and attentive with my lessons, and my gentle teacher had been much pleased with the progress I had made, even in a few days. Her words on the hill had now, however, filled me with anxiety, and I wanted to go a little below the surface of this strange system of life. Why was this large family—twenty-two members present, besides some absent pilgrims, as they are called—composed only of adults? Again, more curious still, why was the father of the house adorned with a majestic beard, while the other men, of various ages, had smooth faces, or, at any rate, nothing more than a slight down on the upper lip and cheeks? It was plain that they never shaved. And were these people all really brothers and sisters? So far, I had been unable, even with the most jealous watching, to detect anything like love-making or flirting; they all treated each other, as Yoletta treated me, with kindness and affection, and nothing more. And if the head of the house was in fact the father of them all—since in two centuries a man might have an indefinite number of children—who was the mother or mothers? I was never good at guessing, but the result of my cogitations was one happy idea—to ask Yoletta whether she had a living mother or not. She was my teacher, my friend and guardian in the house, and if it should turn out that the question was an unfortunate one, an offence, she would be readier to forgive than another.

Accordingly, next day, as soon as we were alone together I put the question to her, although not without a nervous qualm.

She looked at me with the greatest surprise. "Do you mean to say," she answered, "that you do not know I have a mother—that there is a mother of the house?"

"How should I know, Yoletta?" I returned. "I have not heard you address any one as mother; besides, how is one to know anything in a strange place unless he is told?"

"How strange, then, that you never asked till now! There is a mother of the house—the mother of us all, of you since you were made one of us; and it happens, too, that I am her daughter—her only child. You have not seen her because you have never asked to be taken to her; and she is not among us because of her illness. For very long she has been afflicted with a malady from which she cannot recover, and for a whole year she has not left the Mother's Room."

She spoke with eyes cast down, in a low and very sad voice. It was only too plain now that in my ignorance I had been guilty of a grave breach of the etiquette or laws of the house; and anxious to repair my fault, also to know more of the one female in this mysterious community who had loved, or at all events had known marriage, I asked if I might see her.

"Yes," she answered, after some hesitation, still standing with eyes cast down. Then suddenly, bursting into tears, she exclaimed: "Oh, Smith, how could you be in the world and not know that there is a mother in every house! How could you travel and not know that when you enter a house, after greeting the father, you first of all ask to be taken to the mother to worship her and feel her hand on your head? Did you not see that we were astonished and grieved at your silence when you came, and we waited in vain for you to speak?"

I was dumb with shame at her words. How well I remembered that first evening in the house, when I could not but see that something was expected of me, yet never ventured to ask for enlightenment!

Presently, recovering from her tears, she went from the room, and, left alone, I was more than ever filled with wonder at what she had told me. I had not imagined that she had come into the world without a mother; nevertheless, the fact that this passionless girl, who had told me that there was only one kind of love, was the daughter of a woman actually living in the house, of whose existence I had never before heard, except in an indirect way which I failed to understand, seemed like a dream to me. Now I was about to see this hidden woman, and the interview would reveal something to me, for I would discover in her face and conversation whether she was in the same mystic state of mind as the others, which made them seem like the dwellers in some better place than this poor old sinful, sorrowful world. My wishes, however, were not to be gratified, for presently Yoletta returned and said that her mother did not desire to see me then. She looked so distressed when she told me this, putting her white arms about my neck as if to console me for my disappointment, that I refrained from pressing her with questions, and for several days nothing more was spoken between us on the subject.

At length, one day when our lesson was over, with an expression of mingled pleasure and anxiety on her face, she rose and took my hand, saying, "Come."

I knew she was going to take me to her mother, and rose to obey her gladly, for since the conversation I had had with her the desire to know the lady of the house had given me no peace.

Leaving the music-room, we entered another apartment, of the same nave-like form, but vaster, or, at all events, considerably longer. There I started and stood still, amazed at the scene before me. The light, which found entrance through tall, narrow windows, was dim, but sufficient to show the whole room with everything in it, ending at the further extremity at a flight of broad stone steps. The middle part of the floor, running the entire length of the apartment, was about twenty feet wide, but on either side of this passage, which was covered with mosaic, the floor was raised; and on this higher level I saw, as I imagined, a great company of men and women, singly and in groups, standing or seated on great stone chairs in various positions and attitudes. Presently I perceived that these were not living beings, but life-like effigies of stone, the drapery they were represented as wearing being of many different richly-coloured stones, having the appearance of real garments. So natural did the hair look, that only when I ascended the steps and touched the head of one of the statues was I convinced that it was also of stone. Even more wonderful in their resemblance to life were the eyes, which seemed to return my half-fearful glances with a calm, questioning scrutiny I found it hard to endure. I hurried on after my guide without speaking, but when I got to the middle of the room I paused involuntarily once more, so profoundly did one of the statues impress me. It was of a woman of a majestic figure and proud, beautiful face, with an abundance of silvery-white hair. She sat bending forward with her eyes fixed on mine as I advanced, one hand pressed to her bosom, while with the other she seemed in the act of throwing back her white unbound tresses from her forehead. There was, I thought, a look of calm, unbending pride on the face, but on coming closer this expression disappeared, giving place to one so wistful and pleading, so charged with subtle pain, that I stood gazing like one fascinated, until Yoletta took my hand and gently drew me away. Still, in spite of the absorbing nature of the matter on which I was bound, that strange face continued to haunt me, and glancing up and down through that long array of calm-browed, beautiful women, I could see no one that was like it.

Arrived at the end of the gallery, we ascended the broad stone steps, and came to a landing twenty or thirty feet above the level of the floor we had traversed. Here Yoletta pushed a glass door aside and ushered me into another apartment—the Mother's Room. It was spacious, and, unlike the gallery, well-lighted; the air in it was also warm and balmy, and seemed charged with a subtle aroma. But now my whole attention was concentrated on a group of persons before me, and chiefly on its central figure—the woman I had so much desired to see. She was seated, leaning back in a somewhat listless attitude, on a very large, low, couchlike seat, covered with a soft, violet-coloured material. My very first glance at her face revealed to me that she differed in appearance and expression from the other inmates of the house: one reason was that she was extremely pale, and bore on her worn countenance the impress of long-continued suffering; but that was not all. She wore her hair, which fell unbound on her shoulders, longer than the others, and her eyes looked larger, and of a deeper green. There was something wonderfully fascinating to me in that pale, suffering face, for, in spite of suffering, it was beautiful and loving; but dearer than all these things to my mind were the marks of passion it exhibited, the petulant, almost scornful mouth, and the half-eager, half-weary expression of the eyes, for these seemed rather to belong to that imperfect world from which I had been severed, and which was still dear to my unregenerate heart. In other respects also she differed from the rest of the women, her dress being a long, pale-blue robe, embroidered with saffron-coloured flowers and foliage down the middle, and also on the neck and the wide sleeves. On the couch at her side sat the father of the house, holding her hand and talking in low tones to her; two of the young women sat at her feet on cushions, engaged on embroidery work, while another stood behind her; one of the young men was also there, and was just now showing her a sketch, and apparently explaining something in it.

I had expected to find a sick, feeble lady, in a dimly-lighted chamber, with perhaps one attendant at her side; now, coming so unexpectedly before this proud-looking, beautiful woman, with so many about her, I was completely abashed, and, feeling too confused to say anything, stood silent and awkward in her presence.

"This is our stranger, Chastel," said the old man to her, at the same time bestowing an encouraging look on me.

She turned from the sketch she had been studying, and raising herself slightly from her half-recumbent attitude, fixed her dark eyes on me with some interest.

"I do not see why you were so much impressed," she remarked after a while. "There is nothing very strange in him after all."

I felt my face grow hot with shame and anger, for she seemed to look on me and speak of me—not to me—as if I had been some strange, semi-human creature, discovered in the woods, and brought in as a great curiosity.

"No; it was not his countenance, only his curious garments and his words that astonished us," said the father in reply.

She made no answer to this, but presently, addressing me directly, said: "You were a long time in the house before you expressed a wish to see me."

I found my speech then—a wretched, hesitating speech, for which I hated myself—and replied, that I had asked to be allowed to see her as soon as I had been informed of her existence.

She turned on the father a look of surprise and enquiry.

"You must remember, Chastel," said he, "that he comes to us from some strange, distant island, having customs different from ours—a thing I had never heard of before. I can give you no other explanation."

Her lip curled, and then, turning to me, she continued: "If there are houses in your island without mothers in them, it is not so elsewhere in the world. That you went out to travel so poorly provided with knowledge is a marvel to us; and as I have had the pain of telling you this, I must regret that you ever left your own home."

I could make no reply to these words, which fell on me like whip-strokes; and looking at the other faces, I could see no sympathy in them for me; as they looked at her—their mother—and listened to her words, the expression they wore was love and devotion to her only, reminding me a little of the angel faces on Guido's canvas of the "Coronation of the Virgin."

"Go now," she presently added in a petulant tone; "I am tired, and wish to rest"; and Yoletta, who had been standing silently by me all the time, took my hand and led me from the room.

With eyes cast down I passed through the gallery, paying no attention to its strange, stony occupants; and leaving my gentle conductress without a word at the door of the music-room, I hurried away from the house. For I could feel love and compassion in the touch of the dear girl's hand, and it seemed to me that if she had spoken one word, my overcharged heart would have found vent in tears. I only wished to be alone, to brood in secret on my pain and the bitterness of defeat; for it was plain that the woman I had so wished to see, and, since seeing her, so wished to be allowed to love, felt towards me nothing but contempt and aversion, and that from no fault of my own, she, whose friendship I most needed, was become my enemy in the house.

My steps took me to the river. Following its banks for about a mile, I came at last to a grove of stately old trees, and there I seated myself on a large twisted root projecting over the water. To this sequestered spot I had come to indulge my resentful feelings; for here I could speak out my bitterness aloud, if I felt so minded, where there were no witnesses to hear me. I had restrained those unmanly tears, so nearly shed in Yoletta's presence, and kept back by dark thoughts on the way; now I was sitting quietly by myself, safe from observation, safe even from that sympathy my bruised spirit could not suffer.

Scarcely had I seated myself before a great brown animal, with black eyes, round and fierce, rose to the surface of the stream half a dozen yards from my feet; then quickly catching sight of me, it plunged noisily again under water, breaking the clear image reflected there with a hundred ripples. I waited for the last wavelet to fade away, but when the surface was once more still and smooth as dark glass, I began to be affected by the profound silence and melancholy of nature, and by a something proceeding from nature—phantom, emanation, essence, I know not what. My soul, not my sense, perceived it, standing with finger on lips, there, close to me; its feet resting on the motionless water, which gave no reflection of its image, the clear amber sunlight passing undimmed through its substance. To my soul its spoken "Hush!" was audible, and again, and yet again, it said "Hush!" until the tumult in me was still, and I could not think my own thoughts. I could thereafter only listen, breathless, straining my senses to catch some natural sound, however faint. Far away in the dim distance, in some blue pasture, a cow was lowing, and the recurring sound passed me like the humming flight of an insect, then fainter still, like an imagined sound, until it ceased. A withered leaf fell from the tree-top; I heard it fluttering downwards, touching other leaves in its fall until the silent grass received it. Then, as I listened for another leaf, suddenly from overhead came the brief gushing melody of some late singer, a robin-like sound, ringing out clear and distinct as a flourish on a clarionet: brilliant, joyous, and unexpected, yet in keeping with that melancholy quiet, affecting the mind like a spray of gold and scarlet embroidery on a pale, neutral ground. The sun went down, and in setting, kindled the boles of the old trees here and there into pillars of red fire, while others in deeper shade looked by contrast like pillars of ebony; and wherever the foliage was thinnest, the level rays shining through imparted to the sere leaves a translucence and splendour that was like the stained glass in the windows of some darkening cathedral. All along the river a white mist began to rise, a slight wind sprang up and the vapour drifted, drowning the reeds and bushes, and wreathing its ghostly arms about the old trees: and watching the mist, and listening to the "hallowed airs and symphonies" whispered by the low wind, I felt that there was no longer any anger in my heart. Nature, and something in and yet more than nature, had imparted her "soft influences" and healed her "wandering and distempered child" until he could no more be a "jarring and discordant thing" in her sweet and sacred presence.

When I looked up a change had come over the scene: the round, full moon had risen, silvering the mist, and filling the wide, dim earth with a new mysterious glory. I rose from my seat and returned to the house, and with that new insight and comprehension which had come to me—that *message,* as I could not but regard it—I now felt nothing but love and sympathy for the suffering woman who had wounded me with her unmerited displeasure, and my only desire was to show my devotion to her.

XIII

AS I approached the building, soft strains floating far out into the night-air became audible, and I knew that the sweet spirit of music, to which they were all so devoted, was present with them. After listening for a while in the shadow of the portico I went in, and, anxious to avoid disturbing the singers, stole away into a dusky corner, where I sat down by myself. Yoletta had, however, seen me enter, for presently she came to me.

"Why did you not come in to supper, Smith?" she said. "And why do you look so sad?"

"Do you need to ask, Yoletta? Ah, it would have made me so happy if I could have won your mother's affection! If she only knew how much I wish for it, and how much I sympathise with her! But she will never like me, and all I wished to say to her must be left unsaid."

"No, not so," she said. "Come with me to her now: if you feel like that, she will be kind to you—how should it be otherwise?"

I greatly feared that she advised me to take an imprudent step; but she was my guide, my teacher and friend in the house, and I resolved to do as she wished. There were no lights in the long gallery when we entered it again, only the white moonbeams coming through the tall windows here and there lit up a column or a group of statues, which threw long, black shadows on floor and wall, giving the chamber a weird appearance. Once more, when I reached the middle of the room, I paused, for there before me, ever bending forward, sat that wonderful woman of stone, the moonlight streaming full on her pale, wistful face and silvery hair.

"Tell me, Yoletta, who is this?" I whispered. "Is it a statue of some one who lived in this house?"

"Yes; you can read about her in the history of the house, and in this inscription on the stone. She was a mother, and her name was Isarte."

"But why has she that strange, haunting expression on her face? Was she unhappy?"

"Oh, can you not see that she was unhappy! She endured many sorrows, and the crowning calamity of her life was the loss of seven loved sons. They were away in the mountains together, and did not return when expected: for many years she waited for tidings of them. It was conjectured that a great rock had fallen on and crushed them beneath it. Grief for her lost children made her hair white, and gave that expression to her face."

"And when did this happen?"

"Over two thousand years ago."

"Oh, then it is a very old family tradition. But the statue—when was that made and placed here?"

"She had it made and placed here herself. It was her wish that the grief she endured should be remembered in the house for all time, for no one had ever suffered like her; and the inscription, which she caused to be put on the stone, says that if there shall ever come to a mother in the house a sorrow exceeding hers, the statue shall be removed from its place and destroyed, and the fragments buried in the earth with all forgotten things, and the name of Isarte forgotten in the house."

It oppressed my mind to think of so long a period of time during which that unutterably sad face had gazed down on so many generations of the living. "It is most strange!" I murmured. "But do you think it right, Yoletta, that the grief of one person should be perpetuated like that in the house; for who can look on this face without pain, even when it is remembered that the sorrow it expresses ended so many centuries ago?"

"But she was a mother, Smith, do you not understand? It would not be right for us to wish to have our griefs remembered for ever, to cause sorrow to those who succeed us; but a mother is different: her wishes are sacred, and what she wills is right."

Her words surprised me not a little, for I had heard of infallible men, but never of women; moreover, the woman I was now going to see was also a "mother in the house," a successor to this very Isarte. Fearing that I had touched on a dangerous topic, I said no more, and proceeding on our way, we soon reached the Mother's Room, the large glass door of which now stood wide open. In the pale light of the moon—for there was no other in the room—we found Chastel on the couch where I had seen her before, but she was lying extended at full length now, and had only one attendant with her.

Yoletta approached her, and, stooping, touched her lips to the pale, still face. "Mother," she said, "I have brought Smith again; he is anxious to say something to you, if you will hear him."

"Yes, I will hear him," she replied. "Let him sit near me; and now go back, for your voice is needed. And you may also leave me now," she added, addressing the other lady.

The two then departed together, and I proceeded to seat myself on a cushion beside the couch.

"What is it you wish to say to me?" she asked. The words were not very encouraging, but her voice sounded gentler now, and I at once began. "Hush," she said, before I had spoken two words. "Wait until this ends—I am listening to Yoletta's voice."

Through the long, dusky gallery and the open doors soft strains of music were floating to us, and now, mingling with the others, a clearer, bell-like voice was heard, which soared to greater heights; but soon this ceased to be distinguishable, and then she sighed and addressed me again. "Where have you been all the evening, for you were not at supper?"

"Did you know that?" I asked in surprise.

"Yes, I know everything that passes in the house. Reading and work of all kinds are a pain and weariness. The only thing left to me is to listen to what others do or say, and to know all their comings and goings. My life is nothing now but a shadow of other people's lives."

"Then," I said, "I must tell you how I spent the time after seeing you to-day; for I was alone, and no other person can say what I did. I went away along the river until I came to the grove of great trees on the bank, and there I sat until the moon rose, with my heart full of unspeakable pain and bitterness."

"What made you have those feelings?"

"When I heard of you, and saw you, my heart was drawn to you, and I wished above all things in the world to be allowed to love and serve you, and to have a share in your affection; but your looks and words expressed only contempt and dislike towards me. Would it not have been strange if I had not felt extremely unhappy?"

"Oh," she replied, "now I can understand the reason of the surprise your words have often caused in the house! Your very feelings seem unlike ours. No other person would have experienced the feelings you speak of for such a cause. It is right to repent your faults, and to bear the burden of them quietly; but it is a sign of an undisciplined spirit to feel bitterness, and to wish to cast the blame of your suffering on another. You forget that I had reason to be deeply offended with you. You also forget my continual suffering, which sometimes makes me seem harsh and unkind against my will."

"Your words seem only sweet and gracious now," I returned. "They have lifted a great weight from my heart, and I wish I could repay you for them by taking some portion of your suffering on myself."

"It is right that you should have that feeling, but idle to express it," she answered gravely. "If such wishes could be fulfilled my sufferings would have long ceased, since any one of my children would gladly lay down his life to procure me ease."

To this speech, which sounded like another rebuke, I made no reply.

"Oh, this is bitterness indeed—a bitterness you cannot know," she resumed after a while. "For you and for others there is always the refuge of death from continued sufferings: the brief pang of dissolution, bravely met, is nothing in comparison with a lingering agony like mine, with its long days and longer nights, extending to years, and that great blackness of the end ever before the mind. This only a mother can know, since the horror of utter darkness, and vain clinging to life, even when it has ceased to have any hope or joy in it, is the penalty she must pay for her higher state."

I could not understand all her words, and only murmured in reply: "You are young to speak of death."

"Yes, young; that is why it is so bitter to think of. In old age the feelings are not so keen." Then suddenly she put out her hands towards me, and, when I offered mine, caught my fingers with a nervous grasp and drew herself to a sitting position. "Ah, why must I be afflicted with a misery others have not known!" she exclaimed excitedly. "To be lifted above the others, when so young; to have one child only; then after so brief a period of happiness, to be smitten with barrenness, and this lingering malady ever gnawing like a canker at the roots of life! Who has suffered like me in the house? You only, Isarte, among the dead. I will go to you, for my grief is more than I can bear; and it may be that I shall find comfort even in speaking to the dead, and to a stone. Can you bear me in your arms?" she said, clasping me round the neck. "Take me up in your arms and carry me to Isarte."

I knew what she meant, having so recently heard the story of Isarte, and in obedience to her command I raised her from the couch. She was tall, and heavier than I had expected, though so greatly emaciated; but the thought that she was Yoletta's mother, and the mother of the house, nerved me to my task, and cautiously moving step by step through the gloom, I carried her safely to that white-haired, moonlit woman of stone in the long gallery. When I had ascended the steps and brought her sufficiently near, she put her arms about the statue, and pressed its stony lips with hers.

"Isarte, Isarte, how cold your lips are!" she murmured, in low, desponding tones. "Now, when I look into these eyes, which are yours, and yet not yours, and kiss these stony lips, how sorely does the hunger in my heart tempt me to sin! But suffering has not darkened my reason; I know it is an offence to ask anything of Him who gives us life and all good things freely, and has no pleasure in seeing us miserable. This thought restrains me; else I would cry to Him to turn this stone to flesh, and for one brief hour to bring back to it the vanished spirit of Isarte. For there is no one living that can understand my pain; but you would understand it, and put my tired head against your breast, and cover me with your grief-whitened hair as with a mantle. For your pain was like mine, and exceeded mine, and no soul could measure it, therefore in the hunger of your heart you looked far off into the future, where some one would perhaps have a like affliction, and suffer without hope, as you suffered, and measure your pain, and love your memory, and feel united with you, even over the gulf of long centuries of time. You would speak to me of it all, and tell me that the greatest grief was to go away into darkness, leaving no one with your blood and your spirit to inherit the house. This also is my grief, Isarte, for I am barren and eaten up by death, and must soon go away to be where you are. When I am gone, the father of the house will take no other one to his bosom, for he is old, and his life is nearly complete; and in a little while he will follow me, but with no pain and anguish like mine to cloud his serene spirit. And who will then inherit our place? Ah, my sister, how bitter to think of it! for then a stranger will be the mother of the house, and my one only child will sit at her feet, calling her mother, serving her with her hands, and loving and worshipping her with her heart!"

The excitement had now burned itself out: she had dropped her head wearily on my shoulder, and bade me take her back. When I had safely deposited her on the couch again, she remained for some minutes with her face covered, silently weeping.

The scene in the gallery had deeply affected me; now, however, while I sat by her, pondering over it, my mind reverted to that vanished world of sorrow and different social conditions in which I had lived, and where the lot of so many poor suffering souls seemed to me so much more desolate than that of this unhappy lady, who had, I imagined, much to console her. It even seemed to me that the grief I had witnessed was somewhat morbid and overstrained; and, thinking that it would perhaps divert her mind from brooding too much over her own troubles, I ventured, when she had grown calm again, to tell her some of my memories. I asked her to imagine a state of the world and the human family, in which all women were, in one sense, on an equality—all possessing the same capacity for suffering; and where all were, or would be, wives and mothers, and without any such mysterious remedy against lingering pain as she had spoken of. But I had not proceeded far with my picture before she interrupted me.

"Do not say more," she said, with an accent of displeasure. "This, I suppose, is another of those grotesque fancies you sometimes give expression to, about which I heard a great deal when you first came to us. That all people should be equal, and all women wives and mothers seems to me a very disordered and a very repulsive idea. The one consolation in my pain, the one glory of my life, could not exist in such a state as that, and my condition would be pitiable indeed. All others would be equally miserable. The human race would multiply, until the fruits of the soil would be insufficient for its support; and earth would be filled with degenerate beings, starved in body and debased in mind—all clinging to an existence utterly without joy. Life is dark to me, but not to others: these are matters beyond you, and it is presumptuous in one of your condition to attempt to comfort me with idle fancies."

After some moments of silence, she resumed: "The father has said to-day that you came to us from an island where even the customs of the people are different from ours; and perhaps one of their unhappy methods is to seek to medicine a real misery by imagining some impossible and immeasurably greater one. In no other way can I account for your strange words to me; for I cannot believe that any race exists so debased as actually to practise the things you speak of. Remember that I do not ask or desire to be informed. We have a different way; for although it is conceivable that present misery might be mitigated, or forgotten for a season, by giving up the soul to delusions, even by summoning before the mind repulsive and horrible images, that would be to put to an unlawful use, and to pervert, the brightest faculties our Father has given us: therefore we seek no other support in all sufferings and calamities but that of reason only. If you wish for my affection, you will not speak of such things again, but will endeavour to purify yourself from a mental vice, which may sometimes, in periods of suffering, give you a false comfort for a brief season, only to degrade you, and sink you later in a deeper misery. You must now leave me."

This unexpected and sharp rebuke did not anger me, but it made me very sad; for I now perceived plainly enough that no great advantage would come to me from Chastel's acquaintance, since it was necessary to be so very circumspect with her. Deeply troubled, and in a somewhat confused state of mind, I rose to depart. Then she placed her thin, feverish white hand on mine. "You need not go away again," she said, "to indulge in bitter feelings by yourself because I have said this to you. You may come with the others to see me and talk to me whenever I am able to sit here and bear it. I shall not remember your offence, but shall be glad to know that there is another soul in the house to love and honour me."

With such comfort as these words afforded I returned to the music-room, and, finding it empty, went out to the terrace, where the others were now strolling about in knots and couples, conversing and enjoying the lovely moonlight. Wandering a little distance away by myself, I sat down on a bench under a tree, and presently Yoletta came to me there, and closely scrutinised my face.

"Have you nothing to tell me?" she asked. "Are you happier now?"

"Yes, dearest, for I have been spoken to very kindly; and I should have been happier if only——" But I checked myself in time, and said no more to her about my conversation with the mother. To myself I said: "Oh, that island, that island! Why can't I forget its miserable customs, or, at any rate, stick to my own resolution to hold my tongue about them?"

XIV

FROM that day I was frequently allowed to enter the Mother's Room, but, as I had feared, these visits failed to bring me into any closer relationship with the lady of the house. She had indeed forgotten my offence: I was one of her children, sharing equally with the others in her impartial affection, and privileged to sit at her feet to relate to her the incidents of the day, or describe all I had seen, and sometimes to touch her thin white hand with my lips. But the distance separating us was not forgotten. At the two first interviews she had taught me, once for all, that it was for me to love, honour, and serve her, and that anything beyond that—any attempt to win her confidence, to enter into her thoughts, or make her understand my feelings and aspirations—was regarded as pure presumption on my part. The result was that I was less happy than I had been before knowing her: my naturally buoyant and hopeful temper became tinged with melancholy, and that vision of exquisite bliss in the future, which had floated before me, luring me on, now began to look pale, and to seem further and further away.

After my walk with Yoletta—if it can be called a walk—I began to look out for the rainbow lilies, and soon discovered that everywhere under the grass they were beginning to sprout from the soil. At first I found them in the moist valley of the river, but very soon they were equally abundant on the higher lands, and even on barren, stony places, where they appeared latest. I felt very curious about these flowers, of which Yoletta had spoken so enthusiastically, and watched the slow growth of the long, slender buds from day to day with considerable impatience. At length, in a moist hollow of the forest, I was delighted to find the full-blown flower. In shape it resembled a tulip, but was more open, and the colour a most vivid orange yellow; it had a slight delicate perfume, and was very pretty, with a peculiar waxy gloss on the thick petals; still, I was rather disappointed, since the name of "rainbow lily," and Yoletta's words, had led me to expect a many-coloured flower of surpassing beauty.

I plucked the lily carefully, and was taking it home to present it to her, when all at once I remembered that only on one occasion had I seen flowers in her hand, and in the hands of the others, and that was when they were burying their dead. They never wore a flower, nor had I ever seen one in the house, not even in that room where Chastel was kept a prisoner by her malady, and where her greatest delight was to have nature in all its beauty and fragrance brought to her in the conversation of her children. The only flowers in the house were in their illuminations, and those wrought in metal and carved in wood, and the immortal, stony flowers of many brilliant hues in their mosaics. I began to fear that there was some superstition which made it seem wrong to them to gather flowers, except for funeral ceremonies, and afraid of offending from want of thought, I dropped the lily on the ground, and said nothing about it to any one.

Then, before any more open lilies were found, an unexpected sorrow came to me. After changing my dress on returning from the fields one afternoon, I was taken to the hall of judgment, and at once jumped to the conclusion that I had again unwittingly fallen into disgrace; but on arriving at that uncomfortable apartment I perceived that this was not the case. Looking round at the assembled company I missed Yoletta, and my heart sank in me, and I even wished that my first impression had proved correct. On the great stone table, before which the father was seated, lay an open folio, the leaf displayed being only illuminated at the top and inner margin; the coloured part at the top I noticed was torn, the rent extending down to about the middle of the page.

Presently the dear girl appeared, with tearful eyes and flushed face, and advancing hurriedly to the father, she stood before him with downcast eyes.

"My daughter, tell me how and why you did this?" he demanded, pointing to the open volume.

"Oh, father, look at this," she returned, half-sobbing, and touching the lower end of the coloured margin with her finger. "Do you see how badly it is coloured? And I had spent three days in altering and retouching it, and still it displeased me. Then, in sudden anger, I pushed the book from me, and seeing it slipping from the stand I caught the leaf to prevent it from falling, and it was torn by the weight of the book. Oh, dear father, will you forgive me?"

"Forgive you, my daughter? Do you not know how it grieves my heart to punish you; but how can this offence to the house be forgiven, which must stand in evidence against us from generation to generation? For we cease to be, but the house remains; and the writing we leave on it, whether it be good or evil, that too remains for ever. An unkind word is an evil thing, an unkind deed a worse, but when these are repented they may be forgiven and forgotten. But an injury done to the house cannot be forgotten, for it is the flaw in the stone that keeps its place, the crude, inharmonious colour which cannot be washed out with water. Consider, my daughter, in the long life of the house, how many unborn men will turn the leaves of this book, and coming to this leaf will be offended at so grievous a disfigurement! If we of this generation were destined to live for ever, then it might be written on this page for a punishment and warning: 'Yoletta tore it in her anger.' But we must pass away and be nothing to succeeding generations, and it would not be right that Yoletta's name should be remembered for the wrong she did to the house, and all she did for its good forgotten."

A painful silence ensued, then, lifting her tear-stained face, she said, "Oh father, what must my punishment be?"

"Dear child, it will be a light one, for we consider your youth and impulsive nature, and also that the wrong you did was partly the result of accident. For thirty days you must live apart from us, subsisting on bread and water, and holding intercourse with one person only, who will assist you with your work and provide you with all things necessary."

This seemed to me a harsh, even a cruel punishment for so trivial an offence, or accident, rather; but she was not perhaps of the same mind, for she kissed his hand, as if in gratitude for his leniency.

"Tell me, child," he said, putting his hand on her head, and regarding her with misty eyes, "who shall attend you in your seclusion?"

"Edra," she murmured; and the other, coming forward, took her by the hand and led her away.

I gazed eagerly after her as she retired, hungering for one look from her dear eyes before that long separation; but they were filled with tears and bent on the floor, and in a moment she was gone from sight.

The succeeding days were to me dreary beyond description. For the first time I became fully conscious of the strength of a passion which had now become a consuming fire in my breast, and could only end in utter misery—perhaps in destruction—or else in a degree of happiness no mortal had ever tasted before. I went about listlessly, like one on whom some heavy calamity has fallen: all interest in my work was lost; my food seemed tasteless; study and conversation had become a weariness; even in those divine concerts, which fitly brought each tranquil day to its close, there was no charm now, since Yoletta's voice, which love had taught my dull ear to distinguish, no longer had any part in it. I was not allowed to enter the Mother's Room of an evening now, and the exclusion extended also to the others, Edra only excepted; for at this hour, when it was customary for the family to gather in the music-room, Yoletta was taken from her lonely chamber to be with her mother. This was told me, and I also elicited, by means of some roundabout questioning, that it was always in the mother's power to have any person undergoing punishment taken to her, she being, as it were, above the law. She could even pardon a delinquent and set him free if she felt so minded, although in this case she had not chosen to exercise her prerogative, probably because her "sufferings had not clouded her understanding." They were treating her very hardly—father and mother both—I thought in my bitterness.

The gradual opening of the rainbow lilies served only to remind me every hour and every minute of that bright young spirit thus harshly deprived of the pleasure she had so eagerly anticipated. She, above them all, rejoiced in the beauty of this visible world, regarding nature in some of its moods and aspects with a feeling almost bordering on adoration; but, alas! she alone was shut out from this glory which God had spread over the earth for the delight of all his children.

Now I knew why these autumnal flowers were called rainbow lilies, and remembered how Yoletta had told me that they gave a beauty to the earth which could not be described or imagined. The flowers were all undoubtedly of one species, having the same shape and perfume, although varying greatly in size, according to the nature of the soil on which they grew. But in different situations they varied in colour, one colour blending with, or passing by degrees into another, wherever the soil altered its character. Along the valleys, where they first began to bloom, and in all moist situations, the hue was yellow, varying, according to the amount of moisture in different places, from pale primrose to deep orange, this passing again into vivid scarlet and reds of many shades. On the plains the reds prevailed, changing into various purples on hills and mountain slopes; but high on the mountains the colour was blue; and this also had many gradations, from the lower deep cornflower blue to a delicate azure on the summits, resembling that of the forget-me-not and hairbell.

The weather proved singularly favourable to those who spent their time in admiring the lilies, and this now seemed to be almost the only occupation of the inmates, excepting, of course, sick Chastel, imprisoned Yoletta, and myself—I being too forlorn to admire anything. Calm, bright days without a cloud succeeded each other, as if the very elements held the lilies sacred and ventured not to cast any shadow over their mystic splendour. Each morning one of the men would go out some distance from the house and blow on a horn, which could be heard distinctly two miles away; and presently a number of horses, in couples and troops, would come galloping in, after which they would remain all the morning grazing and gambolling about the house. These horses were now in constant requisition, all the members of the family, male and female, spending several hours every day in careering over the surrounding country, seemingly without any particular object. The contagion did not affect me, however, for, although I had always been a bold rider (in my own country), and excessively fond of horseback exercise, their fashion of riding without bridles, and on diminutive straw saddles, seemed to me neither safe nor pleasant.

One morning, after breakfasting, I took my axe, and was proceeding slowly, immersed in thought, to the forest, when hearing a slight swishing sound of hoofs on the grass, I turned and beheld the venerable father, mounted on his charger, and rushing away towards the hills at an insanely break-neck pace. His long garment was gathered tightly round his spare form, his feet drawn up and his head bent far forward, while the wind of his speed divided his beard, which flew out in two long streamers behind. All at once he caught sight of me, and, touching the animal's neck, swept gracefully round in narrowing circles, each circle bringing him nearer, until he came to a stand at my side; then his horse began rubbing his nose on my hand, its breath feeling like fire on my skin.

"Smith," said he, with a grave smile, "if you cannot be happy unless you are labouring in the forest with your axe, you must proceed with your wood-cutting; but I confess it surprises me as much to see you going to work on a day like this, as it would to see you walking inverted on your hands, and dangling your heels in the air."

"Why?" said I, surprised at this speech.

"If you do not know I must tell you. At night we sleep; in the morning we bathe; we eat when we are hungry, converse when we feel inclined, and on most days labour a certain number of hours. But more than these things, which have a certain amount of pleasure in them, are the precious moments when nature reveals herself to us in all her beauty. We give ourselves wholly to her then, and she refreshes us; the splendour fades, but the wealth it brings to the soul remains to gladden us. That must be a dull spirit that cannot suspend its toil when the sun is setting in glory, or the violet rainbow appears on the cloud. Every day brings its special moments to gladden us, just as we have in the house every day our time of melody and recreation. But this supreme and more enduring glory of nature comes only once every year; and while it lasts, all labour, except that which is pressing and necessary, is unseemly, and an offence to the Father of the world." He paused, but I did not know what to say in reply, and presently he resumed: "My son, there are horses waiting for you, and unless you are more unlike us in mind than I ever imagined, you will now take one and ride to the hills, where, owing to the absence of forests, the earth can now be seen at its best."

I was about to thank him and turn back, but the thought of Yoletta, to whom each heavy day now seemed a year, oppressed my heart, and I continued standing motionless, with downcast eyes, wishing, yet fearing, to speak.

"Why is your mind troubled, my son?" he said kindly.

"Father," I answered, that word which I now ventured to use for the first time trembling from my lips, "the beauty of the earth is very much to me, but I cannot help remembering that to Yoletta it is even more, and the thought takes away all my pleasure. The flowers will fade, and she will not see them."

"My son, I am glad to hear these words," he answered, somewhat to my surprise, for I had greatly feared that I had adopted too bold a course. "For I see now," he continued, "that this seeming indifference, which gave me some pain, does not proceed from an incapacity on your part to feel as we do, but from a tender love and compassion—that most precious of all our emotions, which will serve to draw you closer to us. I have also thought much of Yoletta during these beautiful days, grieving for her, and this morning I have allowed her to go out into the hills, so that during this day, at least, she will be able to share in our pleasure."

Scarcely waiting for another word to be spoken, I flew back to the house, anxious enough for a ride now. The little straw saddle seemed now as comfortable as a couch, nor was the bridle missed; for, nerved with that intense desire to find and speak to my love, I could have ridden securely on the slippery back of a giraffe, charging over rough ground with a pack of lions at its heels. Away I went at a speed never perhaps attained by any winner of the Derby, which made the shining hairs of my horse's mane whistle in the still air; down valleys, up hills, flying like a bird over roaring burns, rocks, and thorny bushes, never pausing until I was far away among those hills where that strange accident had befallen me, and from which I had recovered to find the earth so changed. I then ascended a great green hill, the top of which must have been over a thousand feet above the surrounding country. When I had at length reached this elevation, which I did walking and climbing, my steed docilely scrambling up after me, the richness and novelty of the unimaginable and indescribable scene which opened before me affected me in a strange way, smiting my heart with a pain intense and unfamiliar. For the first time I experienced within myself that miraculous power the mind possesses of reproducing instantaneously, and without perspective, the events, feelings, and thoughts of long years—an experience which sometimes comes to a person suddenly confronted with death, and in other moments of supreme agitation. A thousand memories and a thousand thoughts were stirring in me: I was conscious now, as I had not been before, of the past and the present, and these two existed in my mind, yet separated by a great gulf of time—a blank and a nothingness which yet oppressed me with its horrible vastness. How aimless and solitary, how awful my position seemed! It was like that of one beneath whose feet the world suddenly crumbles into ashes and dust, and is scattered throughout the illimitable void, while he survives, blown to some far planet whose strange aspect, however beautiful, fills him with an undefinable terror. And I knew, and the knowledge only intensified my pain, that my agitation, the strugglings of my soul to recover that lost life, were like the vain wing-beats of some woodland bird, blown away a thousand miles over the sea, into which it must at last sink down and perish.

Such a mental state cannot endure for more than a few moments, and passing away, it left me weary and despondent. With dull, joyless eyes I continued gazing for upwards of an hour on the prospect beneath me; for I had now given up all hopes of seeing Yoletta, not yet having encountered a single person since starting for my ride. All about me the summit was dotted with small lilies of a delicate blue, but at a little distance the sober green of the grass became absorbed, as it were, in the brighter flower-tints, and the neighbouring summits all appeared of a pure cerulean hue. Lower down this passed into the purples of the slopes and the reds of the plains, while the valleys, fringed with scarlet, were like rivers of crocus-coloured fire. Distance, and the light, autumnal haze, had a subduing and harmonising effect on the sea of brilliant colour, and further away on the immense horizon it all faded into the soft universal blue. Over this flowery paradise my eyes wandered restlessly, for my heart was restless in me, and had lost the power of pleasure. With a slight bitterness I recalled some of the words the father had spoken to me that morning. It was all very well, I thought, for this venerable greybeard to talk about refreshing the soul with the sight of all this beauty; but he seemed to lose sight of the important fact that there was a considerable difference in our respective ages, that the raging hunger of the heart, which he had doubtless experienced at one time of his life, was, like bodily hunger, not to be appeased with splendid sunsets, rainbows and rainbow lilies, however beautiful they might seem to the eye.

Presently, on a second and lower summit of the long mountain I had ascended, I caught sight of a person on horseback, standing motionless as a figure of stone. At that distance the horse looked no bigger than a greyhound, yet so marvellously transparent was the mountain air, that I distinctly recognised Yoletta in the rider. I started up, and sprang joyfully on to my own horse, and waving my hand to attract her attention, galloped recklessly down the slope; but when I reached the opposing summit she was no longer there, nor anywhere in sight, and it was as if the earth had opened and swallowed her.

XV

DURING Yoletta's seclusion, my education was not allowed to suffer, her place as instructress having been taken by Edra. I was pleased with this arrangement, thinking to derive some benefit from it, beyond what she might teach me; but very soon I was forced to abandon all hope of communicating with the imprisoned girl through her friend and gaoler. Edra was much disturbed at the suggestion; for I did venture to suggest it, though in a tentative, roundabout form, not feeling sure of my ground: previous mistakes had made me cautious. Her manner was a sufficient warning; and I did not broach the subject a second time. One afternoon, however, I met with a great and unexpected consolation, though even this was mixed with some perplexing matters.

One day, after looking long and earnestly into my face, said my gentle teacher to me: "Do you know that you are changed? All your gay spirits have left you, and you are pale and thin and sad. Why is this?"

My face crimsoned at this very direct question, for I knew of that change in me, and went about in continual fear that others would presently notice it, and draw their own conclusions. She continued looking at me, until for very shame I turned my face aside; for if I had confessed that separation from Yoletta caused my dejection, she would know what that feeling meant, and I feared that any such premature declaration would be the ruin of my prospects.

"I know the reason, though I ask you," she continued, placing a hand on my shoulder. "You are grieving for Yoletta—I saw it from the first. I shall tell her how pale and sad you have grown—how different from what you were. But why do you turn your face from me?"

I was perplexed, but her sympathy gave me courage, and made me determined to give her my confidence. "If you know," said I, "that I am grieving for Yoletta, can you not also guess why I hesitate and hide my face from you?"

"No; why is it? You love me also, though not with so great a love; but we *do* love each other, Smith, and you can confide in me."

I looked into her face now, straight into her transparent eyes, and it was plain to see that she had not yet guessed my meaning.

"Dearest Edra," I said, taking her hand, "I love you as much as if one mother had given us birth. But I love Yoletta with a different love—not as one loves a sister. She is more to me than any one else in the world; so much is she that life without her would be a burden. Do you not know what that means?" And then, remembering Yoletta's words on the hills, I added: "Do you not know of more than one kind of love?"

"No," she answered, still gazing enquiringly into my face. "But I know that your love for her so greatly exceeds all others, that it is like a different feeling. I shall tell her, since it is sweet to be loved, and she will be glad to know it."

"And after you have told her, Edra, shall you make known her reply to me?"

"No, Smith; it is an offence to suggest, or even to think, such a thing, however much you may love her, for she is not allowed to converse with any one directly or through me. She told me that she saw you on the hills, and that you tried to go to her, and it distressed her very much. But she will forgive you when I have told her how great your love is, that the desire to look on her face made you forget how wrong it was to approach her."

How strange and incomprehensible it seemed that Edra had so misinterpreted my feeling! It seemed also to me that they all, from the father of the house downwards, were very blind indeed to set down so strong an emotion to mere brotherly affection. I had wished, yet feared, to remove the scales from their eyes; and now, in an unguarded moment, I had made the attempt, and my gentle confessor had failed to understand me. Nevertheless, I extracted some comfort from this conversation; for Yoletta would know how greatly my love exceeded that of her own kindred, and I hoped against hope that a responsive emotion would at last awaken in her breast.

When the last of those leaden-footed thirty days arrived—the day on which, according to my computation, Yoletta would recover liberty before the sun set—I rose early from the straw pallet where I had tossed all night, prevented from sleeping by the prospect of reunion, and the fever of impatience I was in. The cold river revived me, and when we were assembled in the breakfast-room I observed Edra watching me, with a curious, questioning smile on her lips. I asked her the reason.

"You are like a person suddenly recovered from sickness," she replied. "Your eyes sparkle like sunshine on the water, and your cheeks that were so pallid yesterday burn redder than an autumn leaf." Then, smiling, she added these precious words: "Yoletta will be glad to return to us, more on your account than her own."

After we had broken our fast, I determined to go to the forest and spend the day there. For many days past I had shirked wood-cutting; but now it seemed impossible for me to settle down to any quiet, sedentary kind of work, the consuming impatience and boundless energy I felt making me wish for some unusually violent task, such as would exhaust the body and give, perhaps, a rest to the mind. Taking my axe, and the usual small basket of provisions for my noonday meal, I left the house; and on this morning I did not walk, but ran as if for a wager, taking long, flying leaps over bushes and streams that had never tempted me before. Arrived at the scene of action, I selected a large tree which had been marked out for felling, and for hours I hacked at it with an energy almost superhuman; and at last, before I had felt any disposition to rest, the towering old giant, bowing its head and rustling its sere foliage as if in eternal farewell to the skies, came with a mighty crash to the earth. Scarcely was it fallen before I felt that I had laboured too long and violently: the dry, fresh breeze stung my burning cheeks like needles of ice, my knees trembled under me, and the whole world seemed to spin round; then, casting myself upon a bed of chips and withered leaves, I lay gasping for breath, with only life enough left in me to wonder whether I had fainted or not. Recovered at length from this exhausted condition, I sat up, and rejoiced to observe that half the day—that last miserable day—had already flown. Then the thoughts of the approaching evening, and all the happiness it would bring, inspired me with fresh zeal and strength, and, starting to my feet, and taking no thought of my food, I picked up the axe and made a fresh onslaught on the fallen tree. I had already accomplished more than a day's work, but the fever in my blood and brain urged me on to the arduous task of lopping off the huge branches; and my exertions did not cease until once more the world, with everything on it, began revolving like a whirligig, compelling me to desist and take a still longer rest. And sitting there I thought only of Yoletta. How would she look after that long seclusion? Pale, and sad too perhaps; and her sweet, soulful eyes—oh, would I now see in them that new light for which I had watched and waited so long?

Then, while I thus mused, I heard, not far off, a slight rustling sound, as of a hare startled at seeing me, and bounding away over the withered leaves; and lifting up my eyes from the ground, I beheld Yoletta herself hastening towards me, her face shining with joy. I sprang forward to meet her, and in another moment she was locked in my arms. That one moment of unspeakable happiness seemed to out-weigh a hundred times all the misery I had endured. "Oh, my sweet darling—at last, at last, my pain is ended!" I murmured, while pressing her again and again to my heart, and kissing that dear face, which looked now so much thinner than when I had last seen it.

She bent back her head, like Genevieve in the ballad, to look me in the face, her eyes filled with tears—crystal, happy drops, which dimmed not their brightness. But her face was pale, with a pensive pallor like that of the *Gloire de Dijon* rose; only now excitement had suffused her cheeks with the tints of that same rose—that red so unlike the bloom on other faces in vanished days; so tender and delicate and precious above all tints in nature!

"I know," she spoke, "how you were grieving for me, that you were pale and dejected. Oh, how strange you should love me so much!"

"Strange, darling—that word again! It is the one sweetness and joy of life. And are you not glad to be loved?"

"Oh, I cannot tell you how glad; but am I not here in your arms to show it? When I heard that you had gone to the wood I did not wait, but ran here as fast as I could. Do you remember that evening on the hill, when you vexed me with questions, and I could not understand your words? Now, when I love you so much more, I can understand them better. Tell me, have I not done as you wished, and given myself to you, body and soul? How thirty days have changed you! Oh, Smith, do you love me so much?"

"I love you so much, dear, that if you were to die, there would be no more pleasure in life for me, and I should prefer to lie near you underground. All day long I am thinking of you, and when I sleep you are in all my dreams."

She still continued gazing into my face, those happy tears still shining in her eyes, listening to my words; but alas! on that sweet, beautiful face, so full of changeful expression, there was not the expression I sought, and no sign of that maidenly shame which gave to Genevieve in the ballad such an exquisite grace in her lover's eyes.

"I also had dreams of you," she answered. "They came to me after Edra had told me how pale and sad you had grown."

"Tell me one of your dreams, darling."

"I dreamed that I was lying awake on my bed, with the moon shining on me; I was cold, and crying bitterly because I had been left so long alone. All at once I saw you standing at my side in the moonlight. 'Poor Yoletta,' you said, 'your tears have chilled you like winter rain.' Then you kissed them dry, and when you had put your arms about me, I drew your face against my bosom, and rested warm and happy in your love."

Oh, how her delicious words maddened me! Even my tongue and lips suddenly became dry as ashes with the fever in me, and could only whisper huskily when I strove to answer. I released her from my arms and sat down on the fallen tree, all my blissful raptures turned to a great despondence. Would it always be thus—would she continue to embrace me, and speak words that simulated passion while no such feeling touched her heart? Such a state of things could not endure, and my passion, mocked and baffled again and again, would rend me to pieces, and hurl me on to madness and self-destruction. For how many men had been driven by love to such an end, and the women they had worshipped, and miserably died for, compared with Yoletta, were like creatures of clay compared with one of the immortals. And was she not a being of a higher order than myself? It was folly to think otherwise. But how had mortals always fared when they aspired to mate with celestials? I tried then to remember something bearing on this important point, but my mind was becoming strangely confused. I closed my eyes to think, and presently opening them again, saw Yoletta kneeling before me, gazing up into my face with an alarmed expression.

"What is the matter, Smith? you seem ill," she said; and then, laying her fresh palm on my forehead, added: "Your head burns like fire."

"No wonder," I returned. "I'm worrying my brains trying to remember all about them. What were their names, and what did they do to those who loved them—can't you tell me?"

"Oh, you are ill—you have a fever and may die!" she exclaimed, throwing her arms about my neck and pressing her cheek to mine.

I felt a strange imbecility of mind, yet it seemed to anger me to be told that I was ill. "I am not ill," I protested feebly. "I never felt better in my life! But can't you answer me—who were they, and what did they do? Tell me, or I shall go mad."

She started up, and taking the small metal whistle hanging at her side, blew a shrill note that seemed to pierce my brain like a steel weapon. I tried to get up from my seat on the trunk, but only slipped down to the ground. A dull mist and gloom seemed to be settling down on everything; daylight, and hope with it, was fast forsaking the world. But something was coming to us—out of that universal mist and darkness closing around us it came bounding swiftly through the wood—a huge grey wolf! No, not a wolf—a wolf was nothing to it! A mighty, roaring lion crashing through the forest; a monster ever increasing in size, vast and of horrible aspect, surpassing all monsters of the imagination—all beasts, gigantic and deformed, that had ever existed in past geologic ages; a lion with teeth like elephants' tusks, its head clothed as with a black thunder-cloud, through which its eyes glared like twin, blood-red suns! And she—my love—with a cry on her lips, was springing forth to meet it—lost, lost for ever! I struggled frantically to rise and fly to her assistance, and rose, after many efforts, to my knees, only to fall again to the earth, insensible.

XVI

THE violent fever into which I had fallen did not abate until the third day, when I fell into a profound slumber, from which I woke refreshed and saved. I did not, on awakening, find myself in my own familiar cell, but in a spacious apartment new to me, on a comfortable bed, beside which Edra was seated. Almost my first feeling was one of disappointment at not seeing Yoletta there, and presently I began to fear that in the ravings of delirium I had spoken things which had plucked the scales from the eyes of my kind friends in a very rough way indeed, and that the being I loved best had been permanently withdrawn from my sight. It was a blessed relief when Edra, in answer to the questions I put with some heart-quakings to her, informed me that I had talked a great deal in my fever, but unintelligibly, continually asking questions about Venus, Diana, Juno, and many other persons whose names had never before been heard in the house. How fortunate that my crazy brain had thus continued vexing itself with this idle question! She also told me that Yoletta had watched day and night at my side, that at last, when the fever left me, and I had fallen into that cooling slumber, she too, with her hand on mine, had dropped her head on the pillow and fallen asleep. Then, without waking her, they had carried her away to her own room, and Edra had taken her place by my side.

"Have you nothing more to ask?" she said at length, with an accent of surprise.

"No; nothing more. What you have told me has made me very happy—what more can I wish to know?"

"But there is more to tell you, Smith. We know now that your illness is the result of your own imprudence; and as soon as you are well enough to leave your room and bear it, you must suffer the punishment."

"What! Punished for being ill!" I exclaimed, sitting bolt upright in my bed. "What do you mean, Edra? I never heard such outrageous nonsense in my life!"

She was disturbed at this outburst, but quietly and gravely repeated that I must certainly be punished for my illness.

Remembering what their punishments were, I had the prospect of a second long separation from Yoletta, and the thought of such excessive severity, or rather of such cruel injustice, made me wild. "By Heaven, I shall not submit to it!" I exclaimed. "Punished for being ill—who ever heard of such a thing! I suppose that by-and-by it will be discovered that the bridge of my nose is not quite straight, or that I can't see round the corner, and that also will be set down as a crime, to be expiated in solitary confinement, on a bread-and-water diet! No, you shall not punish me; rather than give in to such tyranny I'll walk off and leave the house for ever!"

She regarded me with an expression almost approaching to horror on her gentle face, and for some moments made no reply. Then I remembered that if I carried out that insane threat I should indeed lose Yoletta, and the very thought of such a loss was more than I could endure; and for a moment I almost hated the love which made me so helpless and miserable—so powerless to oppose their stupid and barbarous practices. It would have been sweet then to have felt free—free to fling them a curse, and go away, shaking the dust of their house from my shoes, supposing that any dust had adhered to them. Then Edra began to speak again, and gravely and sorrowfully, but without a touch of austerity in her tone or manner, censured me for making use of such irrational language, and for allowing bitter, resentful thoughts to enter my heart. But the despondence and sullen rage into which I had been thrown made me proof even against the medicine of an admonition imparted so gently, and, turning my face away, I stubbornly refused to make any reply. For a while she was silent, but I misjudged her when I imagined that she would now leave me, offended, to my own reflections.

"Do you not know that you are giving me pain?" she said at last, drawing a little closer to me. "A little while ago you told me that you loved me: has that feeling faded so soon, or do you take any pleasure in wounding those you love?"

Her words, and, more than her words, her tender, pleading tone, pierced me with compunction, and I could not resist. "Edra, my sweet sister, do not imagine such a thing!" I said. "I would rather endure many punishments than give you pain. My love for you cannot fade while I have life and understanding. It is in me like greenness in the leaf—that beautiful colour which can only be changed by sere decay."

She smiled forgiveness, and with a humid brightness in her eyes, which somehow made me think of that joy of the angels over one sinner that repenteth, bent down and touched her lips to mine. "How can you love any one more than that, Smith?" she said. "Yet you say that your love for Yoletta exceeds all others."

"Yes, dear, exceeds all others, as the light of the sun exceeds that of the moon and the stars. Can you not understand that—has no man ever loved you with a love like that, my sister?"

She shook her head and sighed. Did she not understand my meaning now—had not my words brought back some sweet and sorrowful memory? With her hands folded idly on her lap, and her face half averted, she sat gazing at nothing. It seemed impossible that this woman, so tender and so beautiful, should never have experienced in herself, or witnessed in another, the feeling I had questioned her about. But she made no further reply to my words; and as I lay there watching her, the drowsy spirit the fever had left in me overcame my brain, and I slept once more.

For several days, which brought me so little strength that I was not permitted to leave the sick-room, I heard nothing further about my punishment, for I purposely refrained from asking any questions, and no person appeared inclined to bring forward so disagreeable a subject. At length I was pronounced well enough to go about the house, although still very feeble, and I was conducted, not to the judgment-room, where I had expected to be taken, but to the Mother's Room; and there I found the father of the house, seated with Chastel, and with them seven or eight of the others. They all welcomed me, and seemed glad to see me out again; but I could not help remarking a certain subdued, almost solemn air about them, which seemed to remind me that I was regarded as an offender already found guilty, who had now been brought up to receive judgment.

"My son," said the father, addressing me in a calm, judicial tone which at once put my last remaining hopes to flight, "it is a consolation to us to know that your offence is of such a nature that it cannot diminish our esteem for you, or loosen the bonds of affection which unite you to us. You are still feeble, and perhaps a little confused in mind concerning the events of the last few days: I do not therefore press you to give an account of them, but shall simply state your offence, and if I am mistaken in any particular you shall correct me. The great love you have for Yoletta," he continued—and at this I started and blushed painfully, but the succeeding words served to show that I had only too little cause for alarm—"the great love you have for Yoletta caused you much suffering during her thirty days' seclusion from us, so that you lost all enjoyment of life, and eating little, and being in continual dejection, your strength was much diminished. On the last day you were so much excited at the prospect of reunion with her, that you went to your task in the woods almost fasting, and probably after spending a restless night. Tell me if this is not so?"

"I did not sleep that night," I replied, somewhat huskily.

"Unrefreshed by sleep and with lessened strength," he continued, "you went to the woods, and in order to allay that excitement in your mind, you laboured with such energy that by noon you had accomplished a task which, in another and calmer condition of mind and body, would have occupied you more than one day. In thus acting you had already been guilty of a serious offence against yourself; but even then you might have escaped the consequences if, after finishing your work, you had rested and refreshed yourself with food and drink. This, however, you neglected to do; for when you had fallen insensible to the earth, and Yoletta had called the dog and sent it to the house to summon assistance, the food you had taken with you was found untasted in the basket. Your life was thus placed in great peril; and although it is good to lay life down when it has become a burden to ourselves and others, being darkened by that failure of power from which there is no recovery, wantonly or carelessly to endanger it in the flower of its strength and beauty is a great folly and a great offence. Consider how deep our grief would have been, especially the grief of Yoletta, if this culpable disregard of your own safety and well-being had ended fatally, as it came so near ending! It is therefore just and righteous that an offence of such a nature should be recompensed; but it is a light offence, not like one committed against the house, or even against another person, and we also remember the occasion of it, since it was no unworthy motive, but exceeding love, which clouded your judgment, and therefore, taking all these things into account, it was my intention to put you away from us for the space of thirteen days."

Here he paused, as if expecting me to make some reply. He had reproved me so gently, even approving of the emotion, although still entirely in the dark as to its meaning, which had caused my illness, that I was made to feel very submissive, and even grateful to him.

"It is only just," I replied, "that I should suffer for my fault, and you have tempered justice with more mercy than I deserve."

"You speak with the wisdom of a chastened spirit, my son," he said, rising and placing his hand on my head; "and your words gladden me all the more for knowing that you were filled with surprise and resentment when told that your offence was one deserving punishment. And now, my son, I have to tell you that you will not be separated from us, for the mother of the house has willed that your offence shall be pardoned."

I looked in surprise at Chastel, for this was very unexpected: she was gazing at my face with the light of a strange tenderness in her eyes, never seen there before. She extended her hand, and, kneeling before her, I took it in mine and raised it to my lips, and tried, with poor success, to speak my thanks for this rare and beautiful act of mercy. Then the others surrounded me to express their congratulations, the men pressing my hands, but not so the women, for they all freely kissed me; but when Yoletta, coming last, put her white arms about my neck and pressed her lips to mine, the ecstasy I felt was so greatly overbalanced by the pain of my position, and the thought, now almost a conviction, that I was powerless to enlighten them with regard to the nature of the love I felt for her, that I almost shrank from her dear embrace.

XVII

MY attack of illness, although sharp, had passed off so quickly that I confidently looked to complete restoration to my former vigorous state of health in a very short time. Nevertheless, many days went by, and I failed to recover strength, but remained pretty much in that condition of body in which I had quitted the sick-room. This surprised and distressed me at first, but in a little time I began to get reconciled to such a state, and even to discover that it had certain advantages, the chief of which was that the tumult of my mind was over for a season, so that I craved for nothing very eagerly. My friends advised me to do no work; but not wishing to eat the bread of idleness—although the bread was little now, as I had little appetite—I made it a rule to go every morning to the workhouse, and occupy myself for two or three hours with some light, mechanical task which put no strain on me, physical or mental. Even this playing at work fatigued me. Then, after changing my dress, I would repair to the music-room to resume my search after hidden knowledge in any books that happened to be there; for I could read now, a result which my sweet schoolmistress had been the first to see, and at once she had abandoned the lessons I had loved so much, leaving me to wander at will, but without a guide, in that wilderness of a strange literature. I had never been to the library, and did not even know in what part of the house it was situated; nor had I ever expressed a wish to see it. And that for two reasons: one was, that I had already half-resolved—my resolutions were usually of that complexion—never to run the risk of appearing desirous of knowing too much; the other and weightier reason was, that I had never loved libraries. They oppress me with a painful sense of my mental inferiority; for all those tens of thousands of volumes, containing so much important but unappreciated matter, seem to have a kind of collective existence, and to look down on me, like a man with great, staring, owlish eyes, as an intruder on sacred ground—a barbarian, whose proper place is in the woods. It is a mere fancy, I know, but it distresses me, and I prefer not to put myself in the way of it. Once in a book I met with a scornful passage about people with "bodily constitutions like those of horses, and small brains," which made me blush painfully; but in the very next passage the writer makes amends, saying that a man ought to think himself well off if, in the lottery of life, he draws the prize of a healthy stomach without a mind, that it is better than a fine intellect with a crazy stomach. I had drawn the healthy stomach—liver, lungs, and heart to match—and had never felt dissatisfied with my prize. Now, however, it seemed expedient that I should give some hours each day to reading; for so far my conversations and close intimacy with the people of the house had not dissipated the cloud of mystery in which their customs were hid; and by customs I here refer to those relating to courtship and matrimony only, for that was to me the main thing. The books I read, or dipped into, were all highly interesting, especially the odd volumes I looked at belonging to that long series on the *Houses of the World*, for these abounded in marvellous and entertaining matter. There were also histories of the house, and works on arts, agriculture, and various other subjects, but they were not what I wanted.

After three or four hours spent in these fruitless researches, I would proceed to the Mother's Room, where I was now permitted to enter freely every afternoon, and when there, to remain as long as I wished. It was so pleasant that I soon dropped into the custom of remaining until supper-time compelled me to leave it, Chastel invariably treating me now with a loving tenderness of manner which seemed strange when I recalled the extremely unfavourable impression I had made at our first interview.

It was never my nature to be indolent, or to love a quiet, dreamy existence: on the contrary, my fault had lain in the opposite direction, unlimited muscular exercise being as necessary to my well-being as fresh air and good food, and the rougher the exercise the better I liked it. But now, in this novel condition of languor, I experienced a wonderful restfulness both of body and mind, and in the Mother's Room, resting as if some weariness of labour still clung to me, breathing and steeped in that fragrant, summer-like atmosphere, I had long intervals of perfect inactivity and silence, while I sat or reclined, not thinking but in a reverie, while many dreams of pleasures to come drifted in a vague, vaporous manner through my brain. The very character of the room—its delicate richness, the exquisitely harmonious disposition of colours and objects, and the illusions of nature produced on the mind—seemed to lend itself to this unaccustomed mood, and to confirm me in it.

The first impression produced was one of brightness: coming to it by way of the long, dim sculpture gallery was like passing out into the open air, and this effect was partly due to the white and crystal surfaces and the brilliancy of the colours where any colour appeared. It was spacious and lofty, and the central arched or domed portion of the roof, which was of a light turquoise blue, rested on graceful columns of polished crystal. The doors were of amber-coloured glass set in agate frames; but the windows, eight in number, formed the principal attraction. On the glass, hill and mountain scenery was depicted, the summits in some of them appearing beyond wide, barren plains, whitened with the noonday splendour and heat of midsummer, untempered by a cloud, the soaring peaks showing a pearly lustre which seemed to remove them to an infinite distance. To look out, as it were, from the imitation shade of such an arbour, or pavilion, over those far-off, sun-lit expanses where the light appeared to dance and quiver as one gazed, was a never-failing delight. Such was its effect on me, combined with that of the mother's new tender graciousness, resulting I knew not whether from compassion or affection, that I could have wished to remain a permanent invalid in her room.

Another cause of the mild kind of happiness I now experienced was the consciousness of a change in my own mental disposition, which made me less of an alien in the house; for I was now able, I imagined, to appreciate the beautiful character of my friends, their crystal purity of heart and the religion they professed. Far back in the old days I had heard, first and last, a great deal about sweetness and light and Philistines, and not quite knowing what this grand question was all about, and hearing from some of my friends that I was without the qualities they valued most, I thereafter proclaimed myself a Philistine, and was satisfied to have the controversy ended in that way, so far as it concerned me personally. Now, however, I was like one to whom some important thing has been told, who, scarcely hearing and straightway forgetting, goes about his affairs; but, lying awake at night in the silence of his chamber, recalls the unheeded words and perceives their full significance. My sojourn with this people—angelic women and mild-eyed men with downy, unrazored lips, so mild in manner yet in their arts "laying broad bases for eternity"—above all the invalid hours spent daily in the Mother's Room, had taught me how unlovely a creature I had been. It would have been strange indeed if, in such an atmosphere, I had not absorbed a little sweetness and light into my system.

In this sweet refuge—this slumberous valley where I had been cast up by that swift black current that had borne me to an immeasurable distance on its bosom, and with such a change going on within me—I sometimes thought that a little more and I would touch that serene, enduring bliss which seemed to be the normal condition of my fellow-inmates. My passion for Yoletta now burned with a gentle flame, which did not consume, but only imparted an agreeable sense of warmth to the system. When she was there, sitting with me at her mother's feet, sometimes so near that her dark, shining hair brushed against my cheek, and her fragrant breath came on my face; and when she caressed my hand, and gazed full at me with those dear eyes that had no shadow of regret or anxiety in them, but only unfathomable love, I could imagine that our union was already complete, that she was altogether and eternally mine.

I knew that this could not continue. Sometimes I could not prevent my thoughts from flying away from the present; then suddenly the complexion of my dream would change, darkening like a fair landscape when a cloud obscures the sun. Not for ever would the demon of passion slumber and dream in my breast; with recovered strength it would wake again, and, ever increasing in power and ever baffled of its desire, would raise once more that black tempest of the past to overwhelm me. Other darker visions followed: I would see myself as in a magic glass, lying with upturned, ghastly face, with many people about me, hurrying to and fro, wringing their hands and weeping aloud with grief, shuddering at the abhorred sight of blood on their sacred, shining floors; or, worse still, I saw myself shivering in sordid rags and gaunt with long-lasting famine, a fugitive in some wintry, desolate land, far from all human companionship, the very image of Yoletta scorched by madness to formless ashes in my brain; and for all sensations, feelings, memories, thoughts, nothing left to me but a distorted likeness of the visible world, and a terrible unrest urging me, as with a whip of scorpions, ever on and on, to ford yet other black, icy torrents, and tear myself bleeding through yet other thorny thickets, and climb the ramparts of yet other gigantic, barren hills.

But these moments of terrible depression, new to my life, were infrequent, and seldom lasted long. Chastel was my good angel; a word, a touch from her hand, and the ugly spirits would vanish. She appeared to possess a mysterious faculty—perhaps only the keen insight and sympathy of a highly spiritualised nature—which informed her of much that was passing in my heart: if a shadow came there when she had no wish or strength to converse, she would make me draw close to her seat, and rest her hand on mine, and the shadow would pass from me.

I could not help reflecting often and wonderingly at this great change in her manner towards me. Her eyes dwelt lovingly on me, and her keenest suffering, and the unfortunate blundering expressions I frequently let fall, seemed equally powerless to wring one harsh or impatient word from her. I was not now only one among her children, privileged to come and sit at her feet, to have with them a share in her impartial affection; and remembering that I was a stranger in the house, and compared but poorly with the others, the undisguised preference she showed for me, and the wish to have me almost constantly with her, seemed a great mystery.

One afternoon, as I sat alone with her, she made the remark that my reading lessons had ceased.

"Oh yes, I can read perfectly well now," I answered. "May I read to you from this book?" Saying which, I put my hand towards a volume lying on the couch at her side. It differed from the other books I had seen, in its smaller size and blue binding.

"No, not in this book," she said, with a shade of annoyance in her voice, putting out her hand to prevent my taking it.

"Have I made another mistake?" I said, withdrawing my hand. "I am very ignorant."

"Yes, poor boy, you are very ignorant," she returned, placing her hand on my forehead. "You must know that this is a mother's book, and only a mother may read in it."

"I am afraid," I said, with a sigh, "that it will be a long time before I cease to offend you with such mistakes."

"There is no occasion to say that, for you have not offended me, only you make me feel sorry. Every day when you are with me I try to teach you something, to smooth the path for you; but you must remember, my son, that others cannot feel towards you as I do, and it may come to pass that they will sometimes be offended with you, because their love is less than mine."

"But why do you care so much for me?" I asked, emboldened by her words. "Once I thought that you only of all in the house would never love me: what has changed your feelings towards me, for I know that they have changed?" She looked at me, smiling a little sadly, but did not reply. "I think I should be happier for knowing," I resumed, caressing her hand. "Will you not tell me?"

There was a strange trouble on her face as her eyes glanced away and then returned to mine again, while her lips quivered, as if with unspoken words. Then she answered: "No, I cannot tell you now. It would make you happy, perhaps, but the proper time has not yet arrived. You must be patient, and learn, for you have much to learn. It is my desire that you should know all those things concerning the family of which you are ignorant, and when I say all, I mean not only those suitable to one in your present condition, as a son of the house, but also those higher matters which belong to the heads of the house—to the father and mother."

Then, casting away all caution, I answered: "It is precisely a knowledge of those greater matters concerning the family which I have been hungering after ever since I came into the house."

"I know it," she returned. "This hunger you speak of was partly the cause of your fever, and it is in you, keeping you feverish and feeble still; but for this, instead of being a prisoner here, you would now be abroad, feeling the sun and wind on your face."

"And if you know that," I pleaded, "why do you not now impart the knowledge that can make me whole? For surely, all those lesser matters—those things suitable for one in my condition to know—can be learned afterwards, in due time. For they are not of pressing importance, but the other is to me a matter of life and death, if you only knew it."

"I know everything," she returned quickly. But a cloud had come over her face at my concluding words, and a startled look into her eyes. "Life and death! do you know what you are saying?" she exclaimed, fixing her eyes on me with such intense earnestness in them that mine fell abashed before their gaze. Then, after a while, she drew my head down against her knees, and spoke with a strange tenderness. "Do you then find it so hard to exercise a little patience, my son, that you do not acquiesce in what I say to you, and fear to trust your future in my hands? My time is short for all that I have to do, yet I also must be patient and wait, although for me it is hardest. For now your coming, which I did not regard at first, seeing in you only a pilgrim like others—one who through accidents of travel had been cast away and left homeless in the world, until we found and gave you shelter—now, it has brought something new into my life: and if this fresh hope, which is only an old, perished hope born again, ever finds fulfilment, then death will lose much of its bitterness. But there are difficulties in the way which only time, and the energy of a soul that centres all its faculties in one desire, one enterprise, can overcome. And the chief difficulty I find is in yourself—in that strange, untoward disposition so often revealed in your conversation, which you have shown even now; for to be thus questioned and pressed, and to have my judgment doubted, would have greatly offended me in another. Remember this, and do not abuse the privilege you enjoy: remember that you must greatly change before I can share with you the secrets of my heart that concern you. And bear in mind, my son, that I am not rebuking you for a want of knowledge; for I know that for many deficiencies you are not blameworthy. I know, for instance, that nature has denied to you that melodious and flexible voice in which it is our custom every day to render homage to the Father, to express all the sacred feelings of our hearts, all our love for each other, the joy we have in life, and even our griefs and sorrows. For grief is like a dark, oppressive cloud, until from lip and hand it breaks in the rain of melody, and we are lightened, so that even the things that are painful give to life a new and chastened glory. And as with music, so with all other arts. There is a twofold pleasure in contemplating our Father's works: in the first and lower kind you share with us; but the second and more noble, springing from the first, is ours through that faculty by means of which the beauty and harmony of the visible world become transmuted in the soul, which is like a pencil of glass receiving the white sunbeam into itself, and changing it to red, green, and violet-coloured light: thus nature transmutes itself in our minds, and is expressed in art. But in you this second faculty is wanting, else you would not willingly forego so great a pleasure as its exercise affords, and love nature like one that loves his fellow-man, but has no words to express so sweet a feeling. For the happiness of love with sympathy, when made known and returned, is increased an hundredfold; and in all artistic work we commune not with blind, irrational nature, but with the unseen spirit which is in nature, inspiring our hearts, returning love for love, and rewarding our labour with enduring bliss. Therefore it is your misfortune, not your fault, that you are deprived of this supreme solace and happiness."

To this speech, which had a depressing effect on me, I answered sadly: "Every day I feel my deficiencies more keenly, and wish more ardently to lessen the great distance between us; but now—sweet mother, forgive me for saying it!—your words almost make me despond."

"And yet, my son, I have spoken only to encourage you. I know your limitations, and expect nothing beyond your powers; nor do your errors greatly trouble me, believing as I do that in time you will be able to dismiss them from your mind. But the temper of your mind must be changed to be worthy of the happiness I have designed for you. Patience must chasten that reckless spirit in you; for feverish diligence, alternating with indifference or despondence, there must be unremitting effort; and for that unsteady flame of hope, which burns so brightly in the morning and in the evening sinks so low, there must be a bright, unwavering, and rational hope. It would be strange indeed if after this you were cast down; and, lest you forget anything, I will say again that only by giving you enduring happiness and the desire of your heart can my one hope be fulfilled. Consider how much I say to you in these words; it saddens me to think that so much was necessary. And do not think hardly of me, my son, for wishing to keep you a little longer in this prison with me: for in a little while your weakness will pass away like a morning cloud. But for me there shall come no change, since I must remain day and night here with the shadow of death; and when I am taken forth, and the sunshine falls once more on my face, I shall not feel it, and shall not see it, and I shall lie forgotten when you are in the midst of your happy years."

Her words smote on my heart with a keen pain of compassion. "Do not say that you will be forgotten!" I exclaimed passionately; "for should you be taken away, I shall still love and worship your memory, as I worship you now when you are alive."

She caressed my hand, but did not speak; and when I looked up, her worn face had dropped on the pillow, and her eyes were closed. "I am tired—tired," she murmured. "Stay with me a little longer, but leave me if I sleep."

And in a little while she slept. The light was on her face, resting on the purple pillow, and with the soulful eyes closed, and the lips that had no red colour of life in them also closed and motionless, it was like a face carved in ivory of one who had suffered like Isarte in the house and perished long generations ago; and the abundant dark, lustreless hair that framed it, looked dead too, and of the colour of wrought iron.

XVIII

CHASTEL'S words sank deep in my heart—deeper than words had ever sunk before into that somewhat unpromising soil; and although she had purposely left me in the dark with regard to many important matters, I now resolved to win her esteem, and bind her yet more closely to me by correcting those faults in my character she had pointed out with so much tenderness.

Alas! the very next day was destined to bring me a sore trouble. On entering the breakfast-room I became aware that a shadow had fallen on the house. Among his silent people the father sat with grey, haggard face and troubled eyes; then Yoletta entered, her sweet face looking paler than when I had first seen it after her long punishment, while under her heavy, drooping eyelids her skin was stained with that mournful purple which tells of a long vigil and a heart oppressed with anxiety. I heard with profound concern that Chastel's malady had suddenly become aggravated; that she had passed the night in the greatest suffering. What would become of me, and of all those bright dreams of happiness, if she were to die? was my first idea. But at the same time I had the grace to feel ashamed of that selfish thought. Nevertheless, I could not shake off the gloom it had produced in me, and, too distressed in mind to work or read, I repaired to the Mother's Room, to be as near as possible to the sufferer on whose recovery so much now depended. How lonely and desolate it seemed there, now that she was absent! Those mountain landscapes, glowing with the white radiance of mimic sunshine, still made perpetual summer; yet there seemed to be a wintry chill and death-like atmosphere which struck to the heart, and made me shiver with cold. The day dragged slowly to its close, and no rest came to the sufferer, nor sign of improvement to relieve our anxiety. Until past midnight I remained at my post, then retired for three or four miserable, anxious hours, only to return once more when it was scarcely light. Chastel's condition was still unchanged, or, if there had been any change, it was for the worse, for she had not slept. Again I remained, a prey to desponding thoughts, all day in the room; but towards evening Yoletta came to take me to her mother. The summons so terrified me that for some moments I sat trembling and unable to articulate a word; for I could not but think that Chastel's end was approaching. Yoletta, however, divining the cause of my agitation, explained that her mother could not sleep for torturing pains in her head, and wished me to place my hand on her forehead, to try whether that would cause any relief. This seemed to me a not very promising remedy; but she told me that on former occasions they had often succeeded in procuring her ease by placing a hand on her forehead, and that having failed now, Chastel had desired them to call me to her to try my hand. I rose, and for the first time entered that sacred chamber, where Chastel was lying on a low bed placed on a slightly raised platform in the centre of the floor. In the dim light her face looked white as the pillow on which it rested, her forehead contracted with sharp pain, while low moans came at short intervals from her twitching lips; but her wide-open eyes were fixed on my face from the moment I entered the room, and to me they seemed to express mental anguish rather than physical suffering. At the head of the bed sat the father, holding her hand in his; but when I entered he rose and made way for me, retiring to the foot of the bed, where two of the women were seated. I knelt beside the bed, and Yoletta raised and tenderly placed my right hand on the mother's forehead, and, after whispering to me to let it rest very gently there, she also withdrew a few paces.

Chastel did not speak, but for some minutes continued her low, piteous moanings, only her eyes remained fixed on my face; and at last, becoming uneasy at her scrutiny, I said in a whisper: "Dearest mother, do you wish to say anything to me?"

"Yes, come nearer," she replied; and when I had bent my cheek close to her face, she continued: "Do not fear, my son; I shall not die. I cannot die until that of which I have spoken to you has been accomplished."

I rejoiced at her words, yet, at the same time, they gave me pain; for it seemed as though she knew how much my heart had been troubled by that ignoble fear.

"Dear mother, may I say something?" I asked, wishing to tell her of my resolutions.

"Not now; I know what you wish to say," she returned. "Be patient and hopeful always, and fear nothing, even though we should be long divided; for it will be many days before I can leave this room to speak with you again."

So softly had she whispered, that the others who stood so near were not aware that she had spoken at all.

After this brief colloquy she closed her eyes, but for some time the low moans of pain continued. Gradually they sank lower, and became less and less frequent, while the lines of pain faded out of her white, death-like face. And at length Yoletta, stealing softly to my side, whispered, "She is sleeping," and withdrawing my hand, led me away.

When we were again in the Mother's Room she threw her arms about my neck and burst into a tempest of tears.

"Dearest Yoletta, be comforted," I said, pressing her to my breast; "she will not die."

"Oh, Smith, how do you know?" she returned quickly, looking up with her eyes still shining with large drops.

Then, of Chastel's whispered words to me, I repeated those four, "I shall not die," but nothing more; they were, however, a great relief to her, and her sweet, sorrowful face brightened like a drooping flower after rain.

"Ah, she knew, then, that the touch of your hand would cause sleep, that sleep would save her," she said, smiling up at me.

"And you, my darling, how long is it since you closed those sweet eyelids that seem so heavy?"

"Not since I slept three nights ago."

"Will you sit by me here, resting your head on me, and sleep a little now?"

"Not there!" she cried quickly. "Not on the mother's couch. But if you will sit here, it will be pleasant if I can sleep for a little while, resting on you."

I placed myself on the low seat she led me to, and then, when she had coiled herself up on the cushions, with her arms still round my neck, and her head resting on my bosom, she breathed a long happy sigh, and dropped like a tired child to sleep.

How perfect my happiness would have been then, with Yoletta in my arms, clasping her weary little ministering hands in mine, and tenderly kissing her dark, shining hair, but for the fear that some person might come there to notice and disturb me. And pretty soon I was startled to see the father himself coming from Chastel's chamber to us. Catching sight of me he paused, smiling, then advanced, and deliberately sat down by my side.

"This one is sleeping also," he said cheerfully, touching the girl's hair with his hand. "But you need not fear, Smith; I think we shall be able to talk very well without waking her."

I had feared something quite different, if he had only known it, and felt considerably relieved by his words; nevertheless, I was not over-pleased at the prospect of a conversation just then, and should have preferred being left alone with my precious burden.

"My son," he continued, placing a hand on my shoulder, "I sometimes recall, not without a smile, the effect your first appearance produced on us, when we were startled at your somewhat grotesque pilgrim costume. Your attempts at singing, and ignorance of art generally, also impressed me unfavourably, and gave me some concern when I thought about the future—that is, *your* future; for it seemed to me that you had but slender foundations whereon to build a happy life. These doubts, however, no longer trouble me; for on several occasions you have shown us that you possess abundantly that richest of all gifts and safest guide to happiness—the capacity for deep affection. To this spirit of love in you—this summer of the heart which causes it to blossom with beautiful thoughts and deeds—I attribute your success just now, when the contact of your hand produced the long-desired, refreshing slumber so necessary to the mother at this stage of her malady. I know that this is a mysterious thing; and it is commonly said that in such cases relief is caused by an emanation from the brain through the fingers. Doubtless this is so; and I also choose to believe that only a powerful spirit of love in the heart can rightly direct this subtle energy, that where such a spirit is absent the desired effect cannot be produced."

"I do not know," I replied. "Great as my love and devotion is, I cannot suppose it to equal, much less to surpass, that of others who yet failed on this occasion to give relief."

"Yes, yes; only that is looking merely at the surface of the matter, and leaving out of sight the unfathomable mysteries of a being compounded of flesh and spirit. There are among our best instruments peculiar to this house, especially those used chiefly in our harvest music, some of such finely-tempered materials, and of so delicate a construction, that the person wishing to perform on them must not only be inspired with the melodious passion, but the entire system—body and soul—must be in the proper mood, the flesh itself elevated into harmony with the exalted spirit, else he will fail to elicit the tones or to give the expression desired. This is a rough and a poor simile, when we consider how wonderful an instrument a human being is, with the body that burns with thought, and the spirit that quivers and cries with pain, and when we think how its innumerable, complex chords may be injured and untuned by suffering. The will may be ours, but something, we know not what, interposes to defeat our best efforts. That you have succeeded in producing so blessed a result, after we had failed, has served to deepen and widen in our hearts the love we already felt for you; for how much more precious is this melody of repose, this sweet interval of relief from cruel pain the mother now experiences, than many melodies from clear voices and trained hands."

In my secret heart I believed that he was taking much too lofty a view of the matter; but I had no desire to argue against so flattering a delusion, if it were one, and only wished that I could share it with him.

"She is sleeping still," he said presently, "perhaps without pain, like Yoletta here, and her sleep will now probably last for some hours."

"I pray Heaven that she may wake refreshed and free from pain," I remarked.

He seemed surprised at my words, and looked searchingly into my face. "My son," he said, "it grieves me, at a moment like the present, to have to point out a great error to you; but it is an error hurtful to yourself and painful to those who see it, and if I were to pass it over in silence, or put off speaking of it to another time, I should not be fulfilling the part of a loving father towards you."

Surprised at this speech, I begged him to tell me what I had said that was wrong.

"Do you not then know that it is unlawful to entertain such a thought as you have expressed?" he said. "In moments of supreme pain or bitterness or peril we sometimes so far forget ourselves as to cry out to Heaven to save us or to give us ease; but to make any such petition when we are in the full possession of our faculties is unworthy of a reasonable being, and an offence to the Father: for we pray to each other, and are moved by such prayers, remembering that we are fallible, and often err through haste and forgetfulness and imperfect knowledge. But he who freely gave us life and reason and all good gifts, needs not that we should remind him of anything; therefore to ask him to give us the thing we desire is to make him like ourselves, and charge him with an oversight; or worse, we attribute weakness and irresolution to him, since the petitioner thinks by importunity to incline the balance in his favour."

I was about to reply that I had always considered prayer to be an essential part of religion, and not of my form of religion only, but of all religions all over the world. Luckily I remembered in time that he probably knew more about matters "all over the world" than I did, and so held my tongue.

"Have you any doubts on the subject?" he asked, after a while.

"I must confess that I still have some doubts," I replied. "I believe that our Creator and Father desires the happiness of all his creatures and takes no pleasure in seeing us miserable; for it would be impossible not to believe it, seeing how greatly happiness overbalances misery in the world. But he does not come to us in visible form to tell us in an audible voice that to cry out to him in sore pain and distress is unlawful. How, then, do we know this thing? For a child cries to its mother, and a fledgling in the nest to its parent bird; and he is infinitely more to us than parent to child—infinitely stronger to help, and knows our griefs as no fellow-mortal can know them. May we not, then, believe, without hurt to our souls, that the cry of one of his children in affliction may reach him;

that in his compassion, and by means of his sovereign power over nature, he may give ease to the racked body, and peace and joy to the desolate mind?"

"You ask me, How, then, do we know this thing? and you answer the question yourself, yet fail to perceive that you answer it, when you say that although he does not come in a visible form to teach us this thing and that thing, yet we know that he desires our happiness; and to this you might have added a thousand or ten thousand other things which we know. If the reason he gave us to start with makes it unnecessary that he should come to tell us in an audible voice that he desires our happiness, it must also surely suffice to tell us which are lawful and which unlawful of all the thoughts continually rising in our hearts. That any one should question so evident and universally accepted a truth, the foundation of all religion, seems very surprising to me. If it had consisted with his plan to make these delicate mortal bodies capable of every agreeable sensation in the highest degree, yet not liable to accident, and not subject to misery and pain, he would surely have done this for all of us. But reason and nature show us that such an end did not consist with his plan; therefore to ask him to suspend the operations of nature for the benefit of any individual sufferer, however poignant and unmerited the sufferings may be, is to shut our eyes to the only light he has given us. All our highest and sweetest feelings unite with reason to tell us with one voice that he loves us; and our knowledge of nature shows us plainly enough that he also loves all the creatures inferior to man. To us he has given reason for a guide, and for the guidance and protection of the lower kinds he has given instinct: and though they do not know him, it would make us doubt his impartial love for all his creatures, if we, by making use of our reason, higher knowledge, and articulate speech, were able to call down benefits on ourselves, and avert pain and disaster, while the dumb, irrational brutes suffered in silence—the languishing deer that leaves the herd with a festering thorn in its foot; the passage bird blown from its course to perish miserably far out at sea."

His conclusions were perhaps more logical than mine; nevertheless, although I could not argue the matter any more with him, I was not yet prepared to abandon this last cherished shred of old beliefs, although perhaps not cherished for its intrinsic worth, but rather because it had been given to me by a sweet woman whose memory was sacred to my heart—my mother before Chastel.

Fortunately, it was not necessary to continue the discussion any longer, for at this juncture one of the watchers from the sick-room came to report that the mother was still sleeping peacefully, hearing which, the father rose to seek a little needful rest in an adjoining room. Before going, however, he proposed, with mistaken kindness, to relieve me of my burden, and place the girl without waking her on a couch. But I would not consent to have her disturbed; and finally, to my great delight, they left her still in my arms, the father warmly pressing my hand, and advising me to reflect well on his words concerning prayer.

It was growing dark now, and how welcome that obscurity seemed, while with no one nigh to see or hear I kissed her soft tresses a hundred times, and murmured a hundred endearing words in her sleeping ears.

Her waking, which gave me a pang at first, afforded me in the end a still greater bliss.

"Oh, how dark it is—where am I?" she exclaimed, starting suddenly from repose.

"With me, sweetest," I said. "Do you not remember going to sleep on my breast?"

"Yes; but oh, why did you not wake me sooner? My mother—my mother——"

"She is still quietly sleeping, dearest. Ah, I wish you also had continued sleeping! It was such a delight to have you in my arms."

"My love!" she said, laying her soft cheek against mine. "How sweet it was to fall asleep in your arms! When we came in here I could scarcely say a word, for my heart was too full for speech; and now I have a hundred things to say. After all, I should only finish by giving you a kiss, which is more eloquent than speech; so I shall kiss you at once, and save myself the trouble of talking so much."

"Say one of the hundred things, Yoletta."

"Oh, Smith, before this evening I did not think that I could love you more; and sometimes, when I recalled what I once said to you—on the hill, do you remember?—it seemed to me that I already loved you a little too much. But now I am convinced that I was mistaken, for a thousand offences could not alienate my heart, which is all yours for ever."

"Mine for ever, without a doubt, darling?" I murmured, holding her against my breast; and in my rapture almost forgetting that this angelic affection she lavished on me would not long satisfy my heart.

"Yes, for ever, for you shall never, never leave the house. Your pilgrimage, from which you derived so little benefit, is over now. And if you ever attempt to go forth again to find out new wonders in the world, I shall clasp you round with my arms, as I do now, and keep you prisoner against your will; and if you say 'Farewell' a hundred times to me, I shall blot out that sad word every time with my lips, and put a better one in its place, until my word conquers yours."

XIX

ALTHOUGH deprived for the present of all intercourse with Chastel and Yoletta, now in constant attendance on her mother, I ought to have been happy, for all things seemed conspiring to make my life precious to me. Nevertheless, I was far from happy; and, having heard so much said about reason in my late conversations with the father and mother of the house, I began to pay an unusual amount of attention to this faculty in me, in order to discover by its aid the secret of the sadness which continued at all times during this period to oppress my heart. I only discovered, what others have discovered before me, that the practice of introspection has a corrosive effect on the mind, which only serves to aggravate the malady it is intended to cure. During those restful days in the Mother's Room, when I had sat with Chastel, this spirit of melancholy had been with me; but the mother's hallowing presence had given something of a divine colour to it, my passions had slumbered, and, except at rare intervals, I had thought of sorrow as of something at an immeasurable distance from me. Then to my spirit

> "The gushing of the wave
> Far, far away, did seem to mourn and rave
> On alien shores";

and so sweet had seemed that pause, that I had hoped and prayed for its continuance. No sooner was I separated from her than the charm dissolved, and all my thoughts, like evening clouds that appear luminous and rich in colour until the sun has set, began to be darkened with a mysterious gloom. Strive how I might, I was unable to compose my mind to that serene, trustful temper she had desired to see in me, and without which there could be no blissful futurity. After all the admonitions and the comforting assurances I had received, and in spite of reason and all it could say to me, each night I went to my bed with a heavy heart; and each morning when I woke, there, by my pillow, waited that sad phantom, to go with me where I went, to remind me at every pause of an implacable Fate, who held my future in its hands, who was mightier than Chastel, and would shatter all her schemes for my happiness like vessels of brittle glass.

Several days—probably about fifteen, for I did not count them—had passed since I had been admitted into the mother's sleeping-room, when there came an exceedingly lovely day, which seemed to bring to me a pleasant sensation of returning health, and made me long to escape from morbid dreams and vain cravings. Why should I sit at home and mope, I thought; it was better to be active: sun and wind were full of healing. Such a day was in truth one of those captain jewels "that seldom placéd are" among the blusterous days of late autumn, with winter already present to speed its parting. For a long time the sky had been overcast with multitudes and endless hurrying processions of wild-looking clouds—torn, wind-chased fugitives, of every mournful shade of colour, from palest grey to slatey-black; and storms of rain had been frequent, impetuous, and suddenly intermitted, or passing away phantom-like towards the misty hills, there to lose themselves among other phantoms, ever wandering sorrowfully in that vast, shadowy borderland where earth and heaven mingled; and gusts of wind which, as they roared by over a thousand straining trees and passed off with hoarse, volleying sounds, seemed to mimic the echoing thunder. And the leaves—the millions and myriads of sere, cast-off leaves, heaped ankle-deep under the desolate giants of the wood, and everywhere, in the hollows of the earth, lying silent and motionless, as became dead, fallen things—suddenly catching a mock fantastic life from the wind, how they would all be up and stirring, every leaf with a hiss like a viper, racing, many thousands at a time, over the barren spaces, all hurriedly talking together in their dead-leaf language! until, smitten with a mightier gust, they would rise in flight on flight, in storms and stupendous, eddying columns, whirled up to the clouds, to fall to the earth again in showers, and freckle the grass for roods around. Then for a moment, far off in the heavens, there would be a rift, or a thinning of the clouds, and the sunbeams, striking like lightning through their ranks, would illumine the pale blue mist, the slanting rain, the gaunt black boles and branches, glittering with wet, casting a momentary glory over the ocean-like tumult of nature.

In the condition I was in, with a relaxed body and dejected mind, this tempestuous period, which would have only afforded fresh delight to a person in perfect health, had no charm for my spirit; but, on the contrary, it only served to intensify my gloom. And yet day after day it drew me forth, although in my weakness I shivered in the rough gale, and shrank from the touch of the big cold drops the clouds flung down on me. It fascinated me, like the sight of armies contending in battle, or of some tragic action from which the spectator cannot withdraw his gaze. For I had become infected with strange fancies, so persistent and sombre that they were like superstitions. It seemed to me that not I but nature had changed, that the familiar light had passed like a kindly expression from her countenance, which was now charged with an awful menacing gloom that frightened my soul. Sometimes, when straying alone, like an unquiet ghost among the leafless trees, when a deeper shadow swept over the earth, I would pause, pale with apprehension, listening to the many dirge-like sounds of the forest, ever prophesying evil, until in my trepidation I would start and tremble, and look to this side and to that, as if considering which way to fly from some unimaginable calamity coming, I knew not from where, to wreck my life for ever.

This bright day was better suited to my complaint. The sun shone as in spring; not a stain appeared on the crystal vault of heaven; everywhere the unfailing grass gave rest to the eye with its verdure; and a light wind blew fresh and bracing in my face, making my pulses beat faster, although feebly still. Remembering my happy wood-cutting days, before my trouble had come to me, I got my axe and started to walk to the wood; then seeing Yoletta watching my departure from the terrace, I waved my hand to her. Before I had gone far, however, she came running to me, full of anxiety, to warn me that I was not yet strong enough for such work. I assured her that I had no intention of working hard and tiring myself, then continued my walk, while she returned to attend on her mother.

The day was so bright with sunshine that it inspired me with a kind of passing gladness, and I began to hum snatches of old half-remembered songs. They were songs of departing summer, tinged with melancholy, and suggested other verses not meant for singing, which I began repeating.

> "Rich flowers have perished on the silent earth—
> Blossoms of valley and of wood that gave
> A fragrance to the winds."

And again:

> "The blithesome birds have sought a sunnier shore;
> They lingered till the cold cold winds went in
> And withered their green homes."

And these also were fragments, breathing only of sadness, which made me resolve to dismiss poetry from my mind and think of nothing at all. I tried to interest myself in a flight of buzzard-like hawks, soaring in wide circles at an immense height above me. Gazing up into that far blue vault, under which they moved so serenely, and which seemed so infinite, I remembered how often in former days, when gazing up into such a sky, I had breathed a prayer to the Unseen Spirit; but now I recalled the words the father of the house had spoken to me, and the prayer died unformed in my heart, and a strange feeling of orphanhood saddened me, and brought my eyes to earth again.

Half-way to the wood, on an open reach where there were no trees or bushes, I came on a great company of storks, half a thousand of them at least, apparently resting on their travels, for they were all standing motionless, with necks drawn in, as if dozing. They were very stately, handsome birds, clear grey in colour, with a black collar on the neck, and red beak and legs. My approach did not disturb them until I was within twenty yards of the nearest—for they were scattered over an acre of ground; then they rose with a loud, rustling noise of wings, only to settle again at a short distance off.

Incredible numbers of birds, chiefly waterfowl, had appeared in the neighbourhood since the beginning of the wet, boisterous weather; the river too was filled with these new visitors, and I was told that most of them were passengers driven from distant northern regions, which they made their summer home, and were now flying south in search of a warmer climate.

All this movement in the feathered world had, during my troubled days, brought me as little pleasure as the other changes going on about me: those winged armies ever hurrying by in broken detachments, wailing and clanging by day and by night in the clouds, white with their own terror, or black-plumed like messengers of doom, to my distempered fancy only added a fresh element of fear to a nature racked with disorders, and full of tremendous signs and omens.

The interest with which I now remarked these pilgrim storks seemed to me a pleasant symptom of a return to a saner state of mind, and before continuing my walk I wished that Yoletta had been there with me to see them and tell me their history; for she was curious about such matters, and had a most wonderful affection for the whole feathered race. She had her favourites among the birds at different seasons, and the kind she most esteemed now had been arriving for over a month, their numbers increasing day by day until the woods and fields were alive with their flocks.

This kind was named the cloud-bird, on account of its starling-like habit of wheeling about over its feeding-ground, the birds throwing themselves into masses, then scattering and gathering again many times, so that when viewed at a distance a large flock had the appearance of a cloud, growing dark and thin alternately, and continually changing its form. It was somewhat larger than a starling, with a freer flight, and had a richer plumage, its colour being deep glossy blue, or blue-black, and underneath bright chestnut. When close at hand and in the bright sunshine, the aerial gambols of a flock were beautiful to witness, as the birds wheeled about and displayed in turn, as if moved by one impulse, first the rich blue, then the bright chestnut surfaces to the eye. The charming effect was increased by the bell-like, chirping notes they all uttered together, and as they swept round or doubled in the air at intervals came these tempests of melodious sound—a most perfect expression of wild jubilant bird-life. Yoletta, discoursing in the most delightful way about her loved cloud-birds, had told me that they spent the summer season in great solitary marshes, where they built their nests in the rushes; but with cold weather they flew abroad, and at such times seemed always to prefer the neighbourhood of man, remaining in great flocks near the house until the next spring. On this bright sunny morning I was amazed at the multitudes I saw during my walk: yet it was not strange that birds were so abundant, considering that there were no longer any savages on the earth, with nothing to amuse their vacant minds except killing the feathered creatures with their bows and arrows, and no innumerable company of squaws clamorous for trophies—unchristian women of the woods with painted faces, insolence in their eyes, and for ornaments the feathered skins torn from slain birds on their heads.

When I at length arrived at the wood, I went to that spot where I had felled the large tree on the occasion of my last and disastrous visit, and where Yoletta, newly released from confinement, had found me. There lay the rough-barked giant exactly as I had left it, and once more I began to hack at the large branches; but my feeble strokes seemed to make little impression, and becoming tired in a very short time, I concluded that I was not yet equal to such work, and sat myself down to rest. I remembered how, when sitting on that very spot, I had heard a slight rustling of the withered leaves, and looking up beheld Yoletta coming swiftly towards me with outstretched arms, and her face shining with joy. Perhaps she would come again to me to-day: yes, she would surely come when I wished for her so much; for she had followed me out to try to dissuade me from going to the woods, and would be anxiously thinking about me; and she could spare an hour from the sick-room now. The trees and bushes would prevent me from seeing her approach, but I should hear her, as I had heard her before. I sat motionless, scarcely breathing, straining my sense to catch the first faint sound of her light, swift step; and every time a small bird, hopping along the ground, rustled a withered leaf, I started up to greet and embrace her. But she did not come; and at last, sick at heart with hope deferred, I covered my face with my hands, and, weak with misery, cried like a disappointed child.

Presently something touched me, and, removing my hands from my face, I saw that great silver-grey dog which had come to Yoletta's call when I fainted, sitting before me with his chin resting on my knees. No doubt he remembered that last wood-cutting day very well, and had come to take care of me now.

"Welcome, dear old friend!" said I; and in my craving for sympathy of some kind I put my arms over him, and pressed my face against his. Then I sat up again, and gazed into the pair of clear brown eyes watching my face so gravely.

"Look here, old fellow," said I, talking audibly to him for want of something in human shape to address, "you didn't lick my face just now when you might have done so with impunity; and when I speak to you, you don't wag that beautiful bushy tail which serves you for ornament. This reminds me that you are not like the dogs I used to know—the dogs that talked with their tails, caressed with their tongues, and were never over-clean or well-behaved. Where are they now—collies, rat-worrying terriers, hounds, spaniels, pointers, retrievers—dogs rough and dogs smooth; big brute boarhounds, St. Bernards, mastiffs, nearly or quite as big as you are, but not so slender, silky-haired, and sharp-nosed, and without your refined expression of keenness without cunning. And after these canine noblemen of the old *régime*, whither has vanished the countless rabble of mongrels, curs, and pariah dogs; and last of all—being more degenerate—the corpulent, blear-eyed, wheezy pet dogs of a hundred breeds? They are all dead, no doubt: they have been dead so long that I daresay nature extracted all the valuable salts that were contained in their flesh and bones thousands of years ago, and used it for better things—raindrops, froth of the sea, flowers and fruit, and blades of grass. Yet there was not a beast in all that crew of which its master or mistress was not ready to affirm that it could do everything but talk! No one says that of you, my gentle guardian; for dog-worship, with all the ten thousand fungoid cults that sprang up and flourished exceedingly in the muddy marsh of man's intellect, has withered quite away, and left no seed. Yet in intelligence you are, I fancy, somewhat ahead of your far-off progenitors: long use has also given you something like a conscience. You are a good, sensible beast, that's all. You love and serve your master, according to your lights; night and day, you, with your fellows, guard his flocks and herds, his house and fields. Into his sacred house, however, you do not intrude your comely countenance, knowing your place.

"What, then, happened to earth, and how long did that undreaming slumber last from which I woke to find things so altered? I do not know, nor does it matter very much. I only know that there has been a sort of mighty Savonarola bonfire, in which most of the things once valued have been consumed to ashes—politics, religions, systems of philosophy, isms and ologies of all descriptions; schools, churches, prisons, poorhouses; stimulants and tobacco; kings and parliaments; cannon with its hostile roar, and pianos that thundered peacefully; history, the press, vice, political economy, money, and a million things more—all consumed like so much worthless hay and stubble. This being so, why am I not overwhelmed at the thought of it? In that feverish, full age—so full, and yet, my God, how empty!—in the wilderness of every man's soul, was not a voice heard crying out, prophesying the end? I know that a thought sometimes came to me, passing through my brain like lightning through the foliage of a tree; and in the quick, blighting fire of that intolerable thought, all hopes, beliefs, dreams, and schemes seemed instantaneously to shrivel up and turn to ashes, and drop from me, and leave me naked and desolate. Sometimes it came when I read a book of philosophy; or listened on a still, hot Sunday to a dull preacher—they were mostly dull—prosing away to a sleepy, fashionable congregation about Daniel in the lions' den, or some other equally remote matter; or when I walked in crowded thoroughfares; or when I heard some great politician out of office—out in the cold, like a miserable working-man with no work to do—hurling anathemas at an iniquitous government; and sometimes also when I lay awake in the silent watches of the night. A little while, the thought said, and all this will be no more; for we have not found out the secret of happiness, and all our toil and effort is misdirected; and those who are seeking for a mechanical equivalent of consciousness, and those who are going about doing good, are alike wasting their lives; and on all our hopes, beliefs, dreams, theories, and enthusiasms, 'Passing away' is written plainly as the *Mene, mene, tekel, upharsin* by Belshazzar on the wall of his palace in Babylon.

"That withering thought never comes to me now. 'Passing away' is not written on the earth, which is still God's green footstool; the grass was not greener nor the flowers sweeter when man was first made out of clay, and the breath of life breathed into his nostrils. And the human family and race—outcome of all that dead, unimaginable past—this also appears to have the stamp of everlastingness on it; and in its tranquil power and majesty resembles some vast mountain that lifts its head above the clouds, and has its granite roots deep down in the world's centre. A feeling of awe is in me when I gaze on it; but it is vain to ask myself now whether the vanished past, with its manifold troubles and transitory delights, was preferable to this unchanging, peaceful present. I care for nothing but Yoletta; and if the old world was consumed to ashes that she might be created, I am pleased that it was so consumed; for nobler than all perished hopes and ambitions is the hope that I may one day wear that bright, consummate flower on my bosom.

"I have only one trouble now—a wolf that follows me everywhere, always threatening to rend me to pieces with its black jaws. Not you, old friend—a great, gaunt, man-eating, metaphorical wolf, far more terrible than that beast of the ancients which came to the poor man's door. In the darkness its eyes, glowing like coals, are ever watching me, and even in the bright daylight its shadowy form is ever near me, stealing from bush to bush, or from room to room, always dogging my footsteps. Will it ever vanish, like a mere phantom—a wolf of the brain—or will it come nearer and more near, to spring upon and rend me at the last? If they could only clothe my mind as they have my body, to make me like themselves with no canker at my heart, ever contented and calmly glad! But nothing comes from taking thought. I am sick of thought—I hate it! Away with it! I shall go and look for Yoletta, since she does not come to me. Good-bye, old friend, you have been well-behaved and listened with considerable patience to a long discourse. It will benefit you about as much as I have been benefited by many a lecture and many a sermon I was compelled to listen to in the old vanished days."

Bestowing another caress on him I got up and went back to the house, thinking sadly as I walked that the bright weather had not yet greatly improved my spirits.

XX

ARRIVED at the house I was again disappointed at not seeing Yoletta; yet without reasonable cause, since it was scarcely past midday, and she came out from attending on her mother only at long intervals—in the morning, and again just before evening—to taste the freshness of nature for a few minutes.

The music-room was deserted when I went there; but it was made warm and pleasant by the sun shining brightly in at the doors opening to the south. I went on to the extreme end of the room, remembering now that I had seen some volumes there when I had no time or inclination to look at them, and I wanted something to read; for although I found reading very irksome at this period, there was really little else I could do. I found the books—three volumes—in the lower part of an alcove in the wall; above them, within a niche in the alcove, on a level with my face as I stood there, I observed a bulb-shaped bottle, with a long thin neck, very beautifully coloured. I had seen it before, but without paying particular attention to it, there being so many treasures of its kind in the house; now, seeing it so closely, I could not help admiring its exquisite beauty, and feeling puzzled at the scene depicted on it. In the widest part it was encircled with a band, and on it appeared slim youths and maidens, in delicate, rose-coloured garments, with butterfly wings on their shoulders, running or hurriedly walking, playing on instruments of various forms, their faces shining with gladness, their golden hair tossed by the wind—a gay procession, without beginning or end. Behind these joyful ones, in pale grey, and half-obscured by the mists that formed the background, appeared a second procession, hurrying in an opposite direction—men and women of all ages, but mostly old, with haggard, woe-begone faces; some bowed down, their eyes fixed on the ground; others wringing their hands, or beating their breasts; and all apparently suffering the utmost affliction of mind.

Above the bottle there was a deep circular cell in the alcove, about fifteen inches in diameter; fitted in it was a metal ring, to which were attached golden strings, fine as gossamer threads: behind the first ring was a second, and further in still others, all stringed like the first, so that looking into the cell it appeared filled with a mist of golden cobweb.

Drawing a cushioned seat to this secluded nook, where no person passing casually through the room would be able to see me, I sat down, and feeling too indolent to get myself a reading-stand, I supported the volume I had taken up to read on my knees. It was entitled *Conduct and Ceremonial,* and the subject-matter was divided into short sections, each with an appropriate heading. Turning over the leaves, and reading a sentence here and there in different sections, it occurred to me that this might prove a most useful work for me to study, whenever I could bring my mind into the right frame for such a task; for it contained minute instructions upon all points relating to individual conduct in the house—as the entertainment of pilgrims, the dress to be worn, and the conduct to be observed at the various annual festivals, with other matters of the kind. Glancing through it in this rapid way, I soon finished with the first volume, then went through the second in even less time, for many of the concluding sections related to lugubrious subjects which I did not care to linger over; the titles alone were enough to trouble me—Decay through Age, Ailments of Mind and of Body; then Death, and, finally, the Disposal of the Dead. This done I took up the third volume, the last of the series, the first portion of which was headed, *Renewal of the Family.* This part I began to examine with some attention, and pretty soon discovered that I had now at last accidentally stumbled upon a perfect mine of information of the precise kind I had so long and so vainly been seeking. Struggling to overcome my agitation I read on, hurrying through page after page with the greatest rapidity; for there was here much matter that had no special interest for me, but incidentally the things which concerned me most to know were touched on, and in some cases minutely explained. As I proceeded, the prophetic gloom which had oppressed me all that day, and for so many days before, darkened to the blackness of despair, and suddenly throwing up my arms, the book slipped from my knees and fell with a crash upon the floor. There, face downwards, with its beautiful leaves doubled and broken under its weight, it rested unheeded at my feet. For now the desired knowledge was mine, and that dream of happiness which had illumined my life was over. Now I possessed the secret of that passionless, everlasting calm of beings who had for ever outlived, and left as immeasurably far behind as the instincts of the wolf and ape, the strongest emotion of which my heart was capable. For the children of the house there could be no union by marriage; in body and soul they differed from me: they had no name for that feeling which I had so often and so vainly declared; therefore they had told me again and again that there was only one kind of love, for they, alas! could experience one kind only. I did not, for the moment, seek further in the book, or pause to reflect on that still unexplained mystery, which was the very centre and core of the whole matter, namely, the existence of the father and mother in the house, from whose union the family was renewed, and who, fruitful themselves, were yet the parents of a barren race. Nor did I ask who their successors would be: for albeit long-lived, they were mortal like their own passionless children, and in this particular house their lives appeared now to be drawing to an end. These were questions I cared nothing about. It was enough to know that Yoletta could never love me as I loved her—that she could never be mine, body and soul, in my way and not in hers. With unspeakable bitterness I recalled my conversation with Chastel: now all her professions of affection and goodwill, all her schemes for smoothing my way and securing my happiness, seemed to me the veriest mockery, since even she had read my heart no better than the others, and that chill moonlight felicity, beyond which *her* children were powerless to imagine anything, had no charm for my passion-torn heart.

Presently, when I began to recover somewhat from my stupefaction, and to realise the magnitude of my loss, the misery of it almost drove me mad. I wished that I had never made this fatal discovery, that I might have continued still hoping and dreaming, and wearing out my heart with striving after the impossible, since any fate would have been preferable to the blank desolation which now confronted me. I even wished to possess the power of some implacable god or demon, that I might shatter the sacred houses of this later race, and destroy them everlastingly, and repeople the peaceful world with struggling, starving millions, as in the past, so that the beautiful flower of love which had withered in men's hearts might blossom again.

While these insane thoughts were passing through my brain I had risen from my seat, and stood leaning against the edge of the alcove, with that curious richly-coloured bottle close to my eyes. There were letters on it noticed now for the first time—minute, hair-like lines beneath the strange-contrasted processionists depicted on the band—and even in my excited condition I was a little startled when these letters, forming the end of a sentence, shaped themselves into the words—*and for the old life there shall be a new life.*

Turning the bottle round I read the whole sentence. *When time and disease oppress, and the sun grows cold in heaven, and there is no longer any joy on the earth, and the fire of love grows cold in the heart, drink of me, and for the old life there shall be a new life.*

"Another important secret!" thought I; "this day has certainly been fruitful in discoveries. A panacea for all diseases, even for the disease of old age, so that a man may live two hundred years, and still find some pleasure in existence. But for me life has lost its savour, and I have no wish to last so long. There is more writing here—another secret perhaps, but I doubt very much that it will give me any comfort."

When your soul is darkened, so that it is hard to know evil from good, and the thoughts that are in you lead to madness, drink of me, and be cured.

"No, I shall not drink and be cured! Better a thousand times the thoughts that lead to madness than this colourless existence without love. I do not wish to recover from so sweet a malady."

I took the bottle in my hand and unstopped it. The stopper formed a curious little cup, round the rim of which was written, *Drink of me.* I poured some of the liquid out into the cup; it was pale yellow in colour, and had a faint sickly smell as of honeysuckles. Then I poured it back again and replaced the bottle in its niche.

Drink and be cured. No, not yet. Some day, perhaps, my trouble increasing till it might no longer be borne, would drive me to seek such dreary comfort as this cure-all bottle contained. To love without hope was sad enough, but to be without love was even sadder.

I had grown calm now: the knowledge that I had it in my power to escape at once and for ever from that rage of desire, had served to sober my mind, and at last I began to reason about the matter. The nature of my secret feelings could never be suspected, and in the unsubstantial realm of the imagination it would still be in my power to hide myself with my love, and revel in all supreme delight. Would not that be better than this cure—this calm contentment held out to me? And in time also my feelings would lose their present intensity, which often made them an agony, and would come at last to exist only as a gentle rapture stirring in my heart when I clasped my darling to my bosom and pressed her sweet lips with mine. Ah, no! that was a vain dream, I could not be deceived by it; for who can say to the demon of passion in him, thus far shalt thou go and no further?

Perplexed in mind and unable to decide which thing was best, my troubled thoughts at length took me back to that far-off dead past, when the passion of love was so much in man's life. It was much; but in that over-populated world it divided the empire of his soul with a great, ever-growing misery—the misery of the hungry ones whose minds were darkened, through long years of decadence, with a sullen rage against God and man; and the misery of those who, wanting nothing, yet feared that the end of all things was coming to them.

For the space of half an hour I pondered on these things, then said: "If I were to tell a hundredth part of this black retrospect to Yoletta, would not she bid me drink and forget, and herself pour out the divine liquor, and press it to my lips?"

Again I took the bottle with trembling hand, and filled the same small cup to the brim, saying: "For your sake then, Yoletta, let me drink, and be cured; for this is what you would desire, and you are more to me than life or passion or happiness. But when this consuming fire has left me—this feeling which until now burns and palpitates in every drop of my blood, every fibre of my being—I know that you shall still be to me a sweet, sacred sister and immaculate bride, worshipped more of my soul than any mother in the house; that loving and being loved by you shall be my one great joy all my life long."

I drained the cup deliberately, then stopped the bottle and put it back in its place. The liquor was tasteless, but colder than ice, and made me shiver when I swallowed it. I began to wonder whether I would be conscious of the change it was destined to work in me or not; and then, half regretting what I had done, I wished that Yoletta would come to me, so that I might clasp her in my arms with all the old fervour once more, before that icy-cold liquor had done its work. Finally, I carefully raised the fallen book, and smoothed out its doubled leaves, regretting that I had injured it; and, sitting down again, I held the open volume as before, resting on my knees. Now, however, I perceived that it had opened at a place some pages in advance of the passages which had excited me; but, feeling no desire to go back to resume my reading just where I had left off, my eyes mechanically sought the top of the page before me, and this is what I read:

". . . make choice of one of the daughters of the house; it is fitting that she should rejoice for that brighter excellence which caused her to be raised to so high a state, and to have authority over all others, since in her, with the father, all the majesty and glory of the house is centred; albeit with a solemn and chastened joy, like that of the pilgrim who, journeying to some distant tropical region of the earth, and seeing the shores of his native country fading from sight, thinks at one and the same time of the unimaginable beauties of nature and art that fire his mind and call him away, and of the wide distance which will hold him for many years divided from all familiar scenes and the beings he loves best, and of the storms and perils of the great wilderness of waves, into which so many have ventured and have not returned. For now a changed body and soul shall separate her for ever from those who were one in nature with her; and with that superior happiness destined to be hers there shall be the pains and perils of childbirth, with new griefs and cares unknown to those of humbler condition. But on that lesser gladness had by the children of the house in her exaltation, and because there will be a new mother in the house—one chosen from themselves—

there shall be no cloud or shadow; and, taking her by the hand, and kissing her face in token of joy, and of that new filial love and obedience which will be theirs, they shall lead her to the Mother's Room, thereafter to be inhabited by her as long as life lasts. And she shall no longer serve in the house or suffer rebuke; but all shall serve her in love, and hold her in reverence, who is their predestined mother. And for the space of one year she shall be without authority in the house, being one apart, instructing herself in the secret books which it is not lawful for another to read, and observing day by day the directions contained therein, until that new knowledge and practice shall ripen her for that state she has been chosen to fill."

This passage was a fresh revelation to me. Again I recalled Chastel's words, her repeated assurances that she knew what was passing in my mind, that her eyes saw things more clearly than others could see them, that only by giving me the desire of my heart could the one remaining hope of her life be fulfilled. Now I seemed able to understand these dark sayings, and a new excitement, full of the joy of hope, sprang up in me, making me forget the misery I had so recently experienced, and even that increasing sensation of intense cold caused by the draught from the mysterious bottle.

I continued reading, but the above passage was succeeded by minute instructions, extending over several pages, concerning the dress, both for ordinary and extraordinary occasions, to be worn by the chosen daughter during her year of preparation; the conduct to be observed by her towards other members of the family, also towards pilgrims visiting the house in the interval, with many other matters of secondary importance. Impatient to reach the end, I tried to turn the leaves rapidly, but now found that my arm had grown strangely stiff and cold, and seemed like an arm of iron when I raised it, so that the turning over of each leaf was an immense labour. Then I read yet another page, but with the utmost difficulty; for, notwithstanding the eagerness of my mind, my eyes began to remain more and more rigidly fixed on the centre of the leaf, so that I could scarcely force them to follow the lines. Here I read that the bride-elect, her year of preparation being over, rises before daylight, and goes out alone to an appointed place at a great distance from the house, there to pass several hours in solitude and silence, communing with her own heart. Meanwhile, in the house all the others array themselves in purple garments, and go out singing at sunrise to gather flowers to adorn their heads; then, proceeding to the appointed spot, they seek for their new mother, and, finding her, lead her home with music and rejoicing.

When, reading in this miserable, painful way, I had reached the bottom of the page, and attempted to turn it over, I found that I could no longer move my hand—my arms being now like arms of iron, absolutely devoid of sensation, while my hands, rigidly grasping the book like the hands of a frozen corpse, held it upright and motionless before me. I tried to start up and shake off this strange deadness from my body, but was powerless to move a muscle. What was the meaning of this condition? for I had absolutely no pain, no discomfort even; for the sensation of intense cold had almost ceased, and my mind was active and clear, and I could hear and see, and yet was as powerless as if I had been buried in a marble coffin a thousand fathoms deep in earth.

Suddenly I remembered the draught from the bottle, and a terrible doubt shot through my heart. Alas! had I mistaken the meaning of those strange words I had read?—was *death* the cure which that mysterious vessel promised to those who drank of its contents? "When life becomes a burden, it is good to lay it down"; now too late the words of the father, when reproving me after my fever, came back to my mind in all their awful significance.

All at once I heard a voice calling my name, and in a moment the tempest in me was stilled. Yes, it was my darling's voice—she was coming to me—she would save me in this dire extremity. Again and again she called, but the voice now sounded further and further away; and with ineffable anguish I remembered that she would not be able to see me where I sat. I tried to cry out, "Come quick, Yoletta, and save me from death!" but though I mentally repeated the words again and again in an extreme agony of terror, my frozen tongue refused to make a sound. Presently I heard a light, quick step on the floor, then Yoletta's clear voice.

"Oh, I have found you at last!" she cried. "I have been seeking you all over the house. I have something glad to tell you—something to make you happier than on that day—do you remember?—when you saw me coming to you in the wood. The mother has left her chamber at last; she is in the Mother's Room again, waiting impatiently to see you. Come, come!"

Her words sounded distinctly in my ears, and although I could not lift or turn my rigid eyes to see her, yet I seemed to see her now better than ever before, with some fresh glory, as of a new, unaccustomed gladness or excitement enhancing her unsurpassed loveliness, so clearly at that moment did her image shine in my soul! And not hers only, for now suddenly, by a miracle of the mind, the entire family appeared there before me; and in the midst sat Chastel, my sweet, suffering mother, as on that day after my illness when she had pardoned me, and put out her hand for me to kiss. As on that occasion, now—now she was gazing on me with such divine love and compassion in her eyes, her lips half parted, and a slight colour flushing her pale face, recalling to it the bloom and radiance of which cruel disease had robbed her! And in my soul also, at that supreme moment, like a scene starting at the lightning's flash out of thick darkness, shone the image of the house, with all its wide, tranquil rooms rich in art and ancient memories, every stone within them glowing, with everlasting beauty—a house enduring as the green plains and rushing rivers and solemn woods and world-old hills amid which it was set like a sacred gem! O sweet abode of love and peace and purity of heart! O bliss surpassing that of the angels! O rich heritage, must I lose you for ever! Save me from death, Yoletta, my love, my bride—save me—save me—save me!

Then something touched or fell on my neck, and at the same moment a deeper shadow passed over the page before me, with all its rich colouring floating formless, like vapours, mingling and separating, or dancing before my vision, like bright-winged insects hovering in the sunlight; and I knew that she was bending over me, her hand on my neck, her loose hair falling on my forehead.

In that enforced stillness and silence I waited expectant for some moments.

Then a great cry, as of one who suddenly sees a black phantom, rang out loud in the room, jarring my brain with the madness of its terror, and striking as with a hundred passionate hands on all the hidden harps in wall and roof; and the troubled sounds came back to me, now loud and now low, burdened with an infinite anguish and despair, as of voices of innumerable multitudes wandering in the sunless desolations of space, every voice reverberating anguish and despair; and the successive reverberations lifted me like waves and dropped me again, and the waves grew less and the sounds fainter, then fainter still, and died in everlasting silence.

THE END

Lightning Source UK Ltd.
Milton Keynes UK
06 December 2010

163962UK00001B/75/A